Everything about her husband had changed....

Debra tried telling herself it didn't matter, that she didn't care. She didn't want him. But she did. In fact, she ached for him. Over time, she'd come to realize John tried to do what he thought was right. John Richey was a good man.

Every once in a while she would think about how wonderful it would be if they were truly married. Oh, she knew legally they were. But she dreamed of being John's wife, of having the right to touch him when she wanted. And where she wanted.

This was one of those times, and, for the first time since she'd come to his Wyoming ranch, she reveled in her fantasies....

Dear Reader,

I love to write cowboy stories, and when my editor requested I write exactly that, it made me very happy. I think I love cowboys so much because my father and mother were country kids, and visits to my grandparents in the country were a regular occurrence when I was little. Then, in my early teens, I began reading Zane Grey because my mother had the complete set of his books at home. I found them fascinating. I actually began my writing career in the Regency period, writing historical romance, but when I turned to contemporary romances I found my true voice in westerns. I usually set them in Wyoming, which is a place I've visited many times. For those of you who haven't been there, Wyoming is not as large as Texas, my home state, but it's a lot less populated. This works well with Western stories, because in Wyoming you find people still depending on their neighbors for help.

I've always enjoyed marriage-of-convenience stories, too, and that's why I've written this book, *The Rancher Takes a Family*. John doesn't think he will ever find a woman to love again, so decides to embark on a simple marriage of convenience. But things don't go to plan, and his new wife, Debra, soon has him reassessing their situation. As always, love finds a way, and these two discover that they can be a proper family.

I hope you enjoy John and Debra's story, and if you haven't read a Western before, I hope you'll give me and my cowboys a chance. If you have any questions or comments, you can reach me at www.judychristenberry.com.

Happy reading!

Judy Christenberry

JUDY CHRISTENBERRY

The
Rancher
Takes a Family

Western Weddings

SILHOUETTE *Romance*®

Published by Silhouette Books

America's Publisher of Contemporary Romance

 SILHOUETTE BOOKS

ISBN-13: 978-0-373-19830-6
ISBN-10:   0-373-19830-2

THE RANCHER TAKES A FAMILY

First North American Publication 2006

Visit Silhouette Books at www.eHarlequin.com

Printed in U.S.A.

JUDY CHRISTENBERRY

has written over seventy books for Silhouette Books®, and she's a favorite with readers. Now you can find more of Judy's heartwarming and powerful stories in Harlequin Romance®.

Step into a world where family counts, men are true to their word—and where romance always wins the day!

Look out for:

HER CHRISTMAS WEDDING WISH #3919

in November from Harlequin Romance®

RANCHER AND PROTECTOR #3941

On-sale February next year in Harlequin Romance®

CHAPTER ONE

"YOU know we've got to do something, don't you, John?"

John Richey looked at his right-hand man, Bill Hobbs, and sighed. "I know we need to, Bill, but I've thought and thought, and I can't come up with any answer except to just make the best of it."

In spite of his worries he smiled at his baby daughter as he removed the empty bottle from her mouth. She gave him a contented grin worth more than anything money could buy.

Bill persisted. "Damn it, man, we're risking a big loss with just you, me, Mikey and Jess working the ranch, especially since you and me are only working half days so we can take care of Sugar here."

"I told you to call her Betsy. That's her name, after all."

"You're not focusing, John. And I have a solution to our problem even if you don't."

John looked up in surprise. It wasn't the first time they'd had this discussion, but it was the first time Bill had said he had the answer. "What do you mean, you've got the solution? What is it?"

"You won't like it."

John's eyebrows soared. "That's positive."

"Well, you won't. But it's the only way, and it would help someone else out and cure all your ills, too."

"And you've been keeping this miracle to yourself until you thought I was really desperate? I'm beginning to smell a rat, here, Bill."

"I'll tell you what it is if you'll promise to hear me out."

"Okay, I promise." He put Betsy on his shoulder and gently patted her back. Almost immediately, Betsy let out an unladylike burp.

"Good girl," John said with a smile at his nine-month-old daughter.

As if he'd been waiting for that sign, Bill said, "Remember, you promised to hear me out."

"I remember," John said, but his stomach was beginning to churn. Something was bad about Bill's idea.

"You get married again."

John turned to stare at him. "You're crazy, old man! That's not going to happen!"

He stood, with Betsy in his arms, ready to leave the room, but Bill reminded him, "You promised."

"What kind of job is it, Uncle Bill?" Debra Williams asked hesitantly after finally settling herself in his old truck. The day so far had been hectic, what with taking

Andy on his first plane ride—hers, too, for that matter. Even now that they were on terra firma, the trip was still bumpy as the truck bounced along the rutted road to Westlake, Wyoming.

But a rough patch was the least of her worries. Her life had been difficult, but she was a survivor. Always had been. But she wanted more than survival; she wanted to start the life she'd put on hold.

Her dream of being a teacher had been delayed when she'd found herself pregnant in her senior year of high school. Then, when the baby's father died before their son was born, she'd had to face the hard fact that she was the sole support for herself and Andy until he was grown.

For years she'd been doing the best she could, but life hadn't been wonderful.

So when Uncle Bill had called and told her he had a great job for her where she could keep her little boy with her, she accepted his word impulsively.

After she'd picked up the plane tickets and got aboard the flight to Casper, she'd had time to think about what she'd done. She hadn't seen her uncle Bill since she was about six. How much did he know about her life? She knew her mother got letters from him fairly regularly, but that was it, as far as she knew.

Her mother had pleaded for Debra not to take Andy and go. Debra had been surprised and gratified to know that her mother wanted her to stay but she didn't allow such uncharacteristic behavior to influence her decision.

Now, though, she needed reassurance that she'd made the right decision, that what she'd done would help her little boy.

She'd asked a couple of questions earlier, but Uncle Bill had refused to answer her while Andy was awake. Now the three-year-old had finally fallen asleep in his car seat, and she could no longer wait for information. "You know I'm not trained for too many jobs. I was going to go to night school this fall, but you said this was a great job."

"It is, honey, and it will let you stay home with Andy. That's what you want, isn't it?"

"You know it is, Uncle Bill, but there aren't many jobs that will allow that. What do I have to do?"

"Things you already know how to do. Cooking, cleaning, taking care of kids."

"So it's a housekeeping job?"

"Yeah, that's what it is. The thing is, Deb, I can't keep sending you money and—"

"Sending me money? What are you talking about?"

He turned to stare at her until she warned him about an oncoming car. Then he said, "I've been sending your mother money every month to help out. She promised me she was passing it on to you."

Debra looked out the window, unable to face her uncle, knowing that her mother had betrayed her again. They had never had a good relationship. After her father's death, when Debra was nine, her mother had become so self-centered, Debra had practically raised herself. But she hated to think that her mother had intentionally kept money intended to help her own daughter.

She scrambled for a response to her uncle. "I guess she forgot."

Bill slammed the steering wheel. "Damn! I should've known. Eileen was always— Never mind. Things will be better now."

"I hope so," Debra said softly. "I'll certainly work hard. And it will be so wonderful to have Andy with me all day."

Her uncle's revelation explained why her mother had suddenly pleaded with her not to go. Greed had motivated her sudden maternal concern.

As usual, nothing had changed. But knowing the truth destroyed any light of hope that she'd misjudged her mother.

She shook off any sadness, focusing instead on her new life.

"So I'm going to be a housekeeper. How many people are in the family? Are there children Andy can play with?"

"Um, it's a widower and his little girl," Bill mumbled.

"Is there something weird about the job, Uncle Bill?" Something in her uncle's voice didn't seem quite right. She should've known better. There were no fairy-tale happy endings in the world today. She looked back at her sleeping son. She would protect Andy—whatever it took.

"Now, Debbie, honey, I want you to remember I have your best interest at heart."

Debra got a sick feeling in her stomach. She'd pinned her hopes on her uncle's promises. Surely Uncle Bill wouldn't let her down... Would he? She couldn't go back to Kansas City, to living with her mother, to being the cook in a diner, getting up at four-thirty every morning, no matter how she felt. Then she would come home at two, clean house while Andy finished his nap, play with him, fix dinner and go to bed to get up and do it all over again. She was growing old at twenty-two.

What was her uncle's problem? "I don't mind working hard, Uncle Bill."

"Good. 'Cause you'll be working hard." He smiled at her, and she relaxed a little. In his fifties now, her uncle was still a handsome man, tall and muscular, with not a strand of gray in his full head of brown hair. He looked exactly as she remembered him.

They had been passing through mile after mile of ranch land and now she saw a town up ahead. A few shops, a café, a small bank. "Is this Westlake, Uncle Bill?"

Without answering, her uncle pulled to a stop in front of the only other building easily identifiable—a church.

"Uh, Debbie, there's something I haven't told you about the job."

John heard the rear door of the church opening. He glanced over his shoulder from the front pew where he sat holding Betsy and waiting. This was a day he'd remember forever. March second. His second wedding. Guaranteed to be a disaster.

He turned back when he realized Bill was arguing with his niece. Was she hoping for a better deal? After all, his first wife had taught him well. If this one didn't want what he was offering, he'd manage without her.

In fact, this was a dumb idea all-around. He stood, prepared to walk out of the church. Only a crazy man would've given in to Bill's plan. And he wasn't crazy.

The only problem was, he'd have to go past Bill and his niece to get to his truck. And he didn't want to do that.

Suddenly John realized the woman was holding her son. The boy was the only thing about this agreement he liked. Not that he'd ever trade Betsy. True, he'd originally hoped for a boy, but it had only taken a minute of staring down at his tiny baby daughter to win his heart. But he would enjoy having a boy around, too.

It wasn't as if he would ever have a son of his own.

More noise echoed from the rear of the church. He looked over his shoulder again. Bill and his niece were walking to the front. Okay, so she'd finally agreed. Too late to escape now.

"Uh, John," Bill said, sounding nervous, "this here is my niece, Debra Williams, and her boy, Andy."

"Hello," John said. He knew he should offer a smile, but he couldn't. Like a mantra, one line kept repeating in his brain: *This is crazy.... This is crazy....*

As if on cue, a door in the back of the church opened

and the gentle face of their pastor, Reverend Tony Jackson, appeared. He came down the aisle with the big smile of a clergyman who thought he was sending a new couple off to wedded bliss.

"Ah, here's the happy couple. John, introduce me to your lovely bride."

John cleared his throat. "Uh, Reverend Jackson, this is Debra Williams, Bill's niece." He wouldn't exactly call the woman lovely. Especially with that frown. Bill must've just told her about all the work she'd have to do, John figured. Maybe they should halt the proceedings right here and make sure she was willing to do what was necessary.

The reverend shook her hand. "How nice to meet you. Now, if you two will face forward…" He frowned. "Uh, Bill, can you hold the two little ones?"

"Sure, Pastor, I'll just sit here in the front row. After all, I'm the witness, too." He took Betsy out of John's arms and then took the little boy's hand after his mother set him down on the floor.

John's frown deepened. He hated this! After his last marriage, he'd vowed never to marry again. Never to give some woman power over him. And he wasn't including that vulnerability as a part of this marriage. He'd told Bill that.

He finally forced himself to look his new wife in the face. She had brown hair, pale skin, vulnerable gray eyes…

No! He stopped himself with a sharp command. Her

looks didn't matter. He was hiring her! That was how he was going to get through this day, by pretending he was hiring her for a job. Not to be his wife.

"Dearly beloved, we are gathered here today to join this man and this woman in holy matrimony," Reverend Jackson began.

John pressed his lips together, trying to ignore all the wrong things about that statement that seemed to burn a hole in his gut. He felt deceitful—not easy for a man who'd lived an honest life till now.

Before he knew it, the pastor had spoken those terrible words, "I now pronounce you man and wife."

John remembered what would naturally follow those words and he hurriedly said, "Uh, thanks, Reverend Jackson. We'll definitely have you out for dinner after calving season." Then he shoved a white envelope in the man's hand and turned to Bill to get his little girl.

As he reached for Betsy, the shaggy-haired boy looked up at him. Shyly he asked, "Are you a cowboy?"

The question surprised him. He looked down at the blue suit he wore. He'd bought it three years ago when his father died. Not the best memory. He shut it down. "Yeah, I'm a cowboy."

"Not now, Andy," the woman whispered.

Turning to stare at her, John wondered what was so horrible that the little boy wanted to ask. He nodded at Bill. "You'll get them back to the ranch? I'll see you there."

He ignored Bill's protest as he walked out of the church, Betsy in his arms.

Debra watched the man walk away. He was a handsome man, in his late twenties, tall and muscular, with sea-blue eyes. The kind of man any young woman would dream of marrying. Unless she was wise enough to know that looks didn't matter. Her own husband—her first husband, she reminded herself—had been handsome. But he hadn't been much of a husband. Not that John Richey seemed so marriage-minded, either.

She whirled back around to glare at her uncle. "You told me he was happy with this arrangement. That he would be a father to Andy. That he *appreciated* what I was doing!" Those had been the assurances her uncle had given her in the foyer of the church. She knew her son needed a daddy, and it seemed she and John could help each other, as Bill had explained it.

"Now, Debbie, don't get upset. Not in front of Andy," Bill cautioned.

"You lied to me, Uncle Bill," she said in a fierce whisper. "You lured me out here, where I have no way of getting back to Kansas City, and then you lied to me!"

"It's not really like that, Debbie, I swear. He's just angry at—at the idea of marrying again. After all, he's a widower. He needs time, but he don't have any 'cause it's March and calving season is starting and we need someone to take care of Betsy and cook and clean for us. We're out in the saddle almost fifteen hours a day. And that's where you come in."

Debra stared at her uncle as he drew a deep breath. "Then why didn't he just hire me as his housekeeper?"

"'Cause he ain't got no money, honey. He didn't figure no one would work for him unless he could promise them something."

"Uncle Bill, you conned me! If I could, I'd head home right now!"

"You'd take Andy back to that tiny apartment when you can go to a wonderful home? Where he can have a place to play and have you around all day? Come on, Debra! You're a better mother than that. And think about that poor little baby girl, being raised by a couple of cowhands. We hardly know nothing about babies!"

"Oh, give it a rest, Uncle Bill. What's done is done. Take me to my new home and outstanding future opportunity," Debra said with a weary sigh.

Bill helped her and Andy back into his truck and continued on down the road, the small town long gone in the rearview mirror. "I really thought you and John could help each other out. He's just so crazed about getting married, but he'll settle down if you give him a little while."

"What choice do I have?" she asked, not expecting an answer.

They rode in silence until Bill stopped the truck in front of a beautiful house. Debra stared at it in shock.

Having been told that the man didn't have money to pay a housekeeper, she'd expected a tiny log cabin she'd have to share with him and her uncle.

Instead, she was looking at a large, two-story farmhouse-style home with large windows and an inviting front porch. Shade trees along the property made it look welcoming and big enough to house a platoon of soldiers. This was to be her home?

Finally she turned to look at her uncle. "What— I expected— Is this a joke?"

"Only on John," Bill said. When his niece continued to stare at him, he had to explain. "I think he married her too fast, without getting to know her."

"How'd he meet his first wife?" Debra asked.

"At a rodeo in Cheyenne. His dad had just died. He was off balance, needing to be connected to someone. After they got married, she insisted on a new house, new car, jewelry, anything else she could think of. He was in love and he tried to give her everything he could. Especially when he found out she was pregnant."

In a whisper, Debra muttered, "And then she died."

"Not before she ran away with a man who promised to make her a star in Hollywood. She left her two-month-old baby behind without a thought." Bill couldn't keep the anger from his voice. "We got in that evening to hear Betsy bawling. She was wet and hungry. We didn't know what had happened. John almost went crazy until the state highway patrol called."

Debra stared at him in horror.

"Yeah," Bill agreed. "John just about went to pieces. He would have if it hadn't been for Betsy. She needed him."

"I see," Debra said slowly. "John and I have more in common than I'd first thought." Her husband of two months, who'd married her because she was pregnant, even though she was still in high school, gave up his marriage and his job before she got out of high school. His new job choice was drug dealing. He was dead within two weeks.

Bill put a callused hand on hers. "I know. Come on inside."

Inside, the house lived up to its exterior beauty. Almost. Not that there was anything wrong with the inside that a little cleaning wouldn't improve. Debra stared at the family room furnished with three leather couches in a U-shape around a massive stone fireplace. The area was larger than her mother's entire apartment had been.

John came walking into the room from the hallway, holding a piece of paper out to her. "Here's Betsy's schedule. You may choose any of the upstairs bedrooms you want, but stay out of the one down here. It's mine. Dinner should be sometime between seven and eight. There will be four of us at the table in addition to you and the children." He pointed to the rear of the house. "The laundry room is in that direction. Anything you can do there will be appreciated." His voice was calm but challenging, as if he thought she wouldn't be able to do all he asked.

"John—" Bill began, but John didn't wait.

"I'll see you in the barn, Bill," he said and walked out the door.

Debra waited until her uncle turned to look at her, a helpless expression on his face. "It's all right, Uncle Bill. I told you I'd work hard. And I realize we're both in a situation that we now can't change." She straightened her spine and looked around. "How big a ranch is this?"

"It's not all that big. Fifteen thousand acres. That's—" He hung his head, fingering the hat he held in his hands. Without looking up, he said, "We needed help. Debbie, I swear, if you'll give him a little time—"

"He's got all the time in the world until I can find a way to make enough money to get me and my son back home."

Debra investigated the house and determined the two bedrooms she and Andy would take upstairs.

The third bedroom, next to hers, was occupied by a sleeping baby. Debra stood at the crib, looking down at Betsy. The blond-haired child was so sweet. Babies always were.

Debra smiled, remembering Andy's younger years. Then she heard her son calling her and rushed out of the baby's room to keep him from awakening Betsy.

"Do you like your room, Andy?" she asked.

"It's big, Mommy. I think I'd rather stay with you."

She put her arms around him. "You'll be right next door to me, baby. And it means you can sleep later without me waking you up. You'll get used to it, I promise." She hugged him tighter. "How 'bout we go to the kitchen and see if we can find you a snack?"

Downstairs she discovered a beautiful kitchen, complete with all the latest appliances. Since she was a short-order cook, she appreciated the convenience of a large, modern kitchen. The one good thing she could say about the job at Joe's Diner was that it had allowed her to spend the late afternoons and evenings with Andy. Of course, she'd had to go to bed when he did since she got up at four-thirty in the morning to go to work. Her entire paycheck went to her mother. Eileen demanded money for letting them live with her, money for taking care of Andy. Money for everything.

The only money Debra had secreted away was her share of the tip money that Joe, the owner, had given her at the end of each month. It hadn't come to much, but it allowed her to buy Andy clothes and occasionally treat him to something special.

She should've saved it so she could get back to Kansas.

Then she stopped to consider her own words. Did she want to go back? Did she want that life? She shuddered. The answer was no. She probably wouldn't be the man's wife for long, but at least she would have some respite from having to abandon her son every morning. And

God knew, she couldn't go back to living with her mother, not knowing what she did now.

"Mommy?"

"Oh, yes, honey, I'm sorry. Let's go find that snack."

She'd assumed she'd find the cupboard bare if this man—her new husband—was so broke he couldn't pay for anyone to help him. However, she found his penniless state didn't apply to the kitchen. The refrigerator was stocked and a nearby freezer was full of frozen beef.

Checking the clock, she removed some meat for the evening dinner she was expected to prepare. Then she found some crackers and peanut butter for Andy.

"I like peanut butter," he said, smiling for the first time since they'd gotten off the plane in Casper that morning.

"I know you do, sweetheart."

"Eileen didn't like to give me peanut butter," Andy muttered. Her mother had insisted Andy call her by her first name so people wouldn't realize she was a grandmother.

Debra leaned over to brush back a wisp of Andy's hair. "I know, sweetie. That's one good thing about living here. No Eileen."

"Really?"

"Really, Andy. You get to stay home with me and your new sister, Betsy."

He frowned. "But she's a girl."

She couldn't stifle a laugh. "So am I, young man.

You'll grow to love Betsy. Her daddy says she'll be up soon and then you'll really get to meet her. You'll see. It will be great."

As Andy ate, Debra moved about the kitchen, locating equipment and ingredients, mentally inventorying the pantry, that was well organized. If John's wife had done all this, she must have been a good cook.

In the monitor on the table Debra heard the sound of a baby stirring.

"Betsy's awake," she told Andy. "Wait here and I'll go get her."

When she entered the baby's room, Betsy was standing in her bed, holding on to the rails, beginning to get unhappy. Debra crossed over to her and picked her up. "Hello, there, Betsy. I'm your new mommy. Let's see. Ah, yes, you need a diaper change, don't you?"

She laid the baby down in her crib and found a clean diaper in the holder at the end. "Your daddy has everything organized, doesn't he? He must be a good daddy, Betsy."

And that was the first thing she found to like about John Richey.

John rushed as he rubbed down his horse. "Sorry, Beauty, but I'm in a hurry," he whispered.

"Did you say something, boss?" Mikey asked, peering around the dark horse John was working on.

"Uh, no, Mikey, nothing." Mikey was young, but a hard worker.

"You sure the missus don't mind us coming to the house for dinner tonight?" Jess, his other cowhand, asked.

John hurriedly looked away from Bill's worried frown. "I'm sure. I told her we'd all four be there. But I don't know what kind of cook she is, so blame Bill if it's awful." He figured even Jess wouldn't have the nerve to question Bill. Both guys were just a little afraid of him.

"Can't be worse than our cooking," Jess grumbled.

"I'm sure Debra will have a good meal ready," Bill said with bravado. "I mean, she used to be a cook. How bad can it be?"

"I'm hungry enough to eat a bear, so let's just hurry," Mikey said.

All four men walked to the house together. John was beginning to wish he hadn't planned on all of them coming to the house to eat this evening. He was beginning to fear that the woman might have done nothing just to pay him back for his rudeness to her earlier. She could completely humiliate him.

Betsy.

He'd walked out on Betsy and left her with a stranger. That thought hadn't struck him until just now.

How could he have done that? Betsy was the most important part of his life. And he'd trusted her to his new wife.

Speeding up, he reached the house before his men.

When he entered, he ignored the warm fire in the fireplace, the delicious aroma in the air, the place settings on the table. All he could think of was his child.

When Debra walked out of the kitchen, all he said was, "Where's Betsy?"

CHAPTER TWO

"SHE'S already in bed. Is there a problem?"

Debra stared at John's worried face. Had she done something wrong?

"I'll go check on her," he said.

She stepped in his way. "I thought maybe you'd all like to shower and change into clean clothes before dinner."

"What's wrong? Don't we smell pretty enough for you?"

Her back stiffened, but her voice remained calm. "I was only thinking of your comfort."

"Well, I might have clean clothes here, but the others don't," he snapped.

She already knew the answer to her question, but she let her eyes widen with innocence. "You mean all the laundry I did today was yours?"

He started to speak but promptly shut his mouth and stared at her. Finally he said, "You did all the laundry today?"

"Yes." She walked into the mudroom where she heard the other cowboys and her uncle. She told the men, "I divided the clothes into stacks by size, since I didn't know what belonged to each of you." She gestured toward the shower stall. "I thought you might be more comfortable if you showered and dressed in clean clothes that you could put on again in the morning and work in. Does that seem like a good idea to you?" Without awaiting their answer, she continued. "And while you're doing that, I'll put dinner on the table."

The men all nodded and immediately grabbed their clean clothes. Debra delicately withdrew and pulled the door behind her. Only John was on this side of the door.

He stood there against the wall, his arms crossed over his wide chest, his blue eyes narrowed to mere slits. "Very clever of you, getting them on your side."

Swallowing a retort, she turned her back on him and walked into the kitchen.

Once there, she drew a deep breath. She'd worked hard all day, but it was work she loved. The best part was that she'd had Andy and Betsy for company. The entire day had been so much better than her life in Kansas that she'd decided the thing to do was to make the best of the situation and see where it led.

But John apparently wasn't going to make it easy.

She began putting the meal on the table. The centerpiece was a giant roast beef she'd cooked until tender, flanked by bowls of gravy, homemade biscuits, whipped potatoes, broccoli and red beans.

Just as everything was in place, the door to the mudroom opened and four men emerged. She moved to the kitchen door and extended her hand to the two men she hadn't formally met. They were both young, in their early twenties, but they looked strong. "Hello, I'm Debra. Welcome to my kitchen," she said with a smile.

The men introduced themselves, but she could tell they were distracted by the large amounts of food ready for them. All she did was nod in the direction of the table and the four men took their seats and dug in, no doubt ravenous after their workday.

"Man, this is the best food I've ever eaten, Miz Richey."

"Thank you, Mikey, but please, call me Debra."

"I'll call you anything you want for a meal like this," the cowboy returned.

"Debra will be fine, Mikey," she said through a smile.

"Thank you for the clean clothes, too," Jess added between bites.

"My pleasure. If you're in the saddle all day, I don't see how you've managed to get anything else done. I'd be exhausted."

"True," Jess said as he buttered a biscuit. "And we're mighty grateful to you."

Those two were completely won over, Debra thought. Unfortunately, her husband wasn't. She noted that John's face was growing stormier every moment. He obviously hadn't counted on her doing her job. He'd immediately gone up to check on Betsy before his shower. Did he think she hadn't taken care of her? Who could resist such a sweet baby?

When the men had finished, Debra asked if they'd like a roast beef sandwich to take with them in the morning, since they didn't come in for lunch. She immediately got a pleased reception to her idea.

John, however, said, "Maybe you don't realize that you have to have breakfast ready at six."

"I assumed you started to work early, John," she said calmly.

"My idea of 'early' isn't nine o'clock."

She ignored the sarcasm in his voice. "For the last three years I've been getting up at four-thirty for work, so six o'clock will be sleeping in for me." Take that, cowboy! She punctuated her reply with a verbal punch but kept it to herself. This man certainly had a lot to learn if he thought she'd run screaming from hard work.

John was quiet as she cleared the table and put a homemade chocolate cake in the middle. "Would anyone care for dessert?" she asked, her voice as sweet as the frosting.

Not even John said no. He didn't, however, join the men in their rousing praise for her good cooking.

When she began the cleanup, the men actually brought their dishes to the sink, a courtesy she hadn't expected. She warmly thanked them and suggested they go to the family room and relax.

With the dishwasher, the cleanup only took a few minutes. She swept the floor and wiped down the counters, then performed a visual check to be sure the kitchen was immaculate before she went to the mudroom to launder their dirty clothes.

As she was loading the washing machine, she felt someone staring at her. Spinning around, she found John at the door.

"You don't have to do that tonight. You've already worked hard enough." He glanced away from her as he spoke.

"Actually, the machine does all the work...unless the noise will bother you."

"No, but—" He kept his head down, as if the toes of his boots were worthy of intense study. "Listen, I was rude this morning. You did all the work anyway. I owe you an apology."

So there was a human under all that bluster, she thought, barely suppressing a smile. Maybe Uncle Bill was right and John just needed some time to get used to the idea of marriage again. And, she had to admit, it felt good to be appreciated for what she'd done. No one had ever made her feel that way, especially her mother.

"I think Uncle Bill may have misled both of us," she said. "But now you know I'm a hard worker, and I appreciate the benefits."

Something she'd said upset him, she realized at once. His head shot up and his back stiffened. Before she could inquire, he turned back on those boot heels and walked away.

Debra stood there, laundry in hand. What had she said to chase away the new and improved John Richey? Whatever it was, it had cost her an opportunity to make peace with her new husband, and she regretted it. When, she wondered, would she get another chance?

John appreciated the well-cooked meal and the clean clothes, but that didn't reconcile him to his second marriage. Especially since his new wife was counting on reaping the "benefits." So she thought she could get a lot of nice things out of him like Elizabeth had? Well, she thought wrong.

Betsy seemed at peace, too. She was clean and sweet-smelling and sound asleep. Still, she'd wake up at four in the morning, as usual, and he'd feed her the 4:00 a.m. bottle, as usual. He loved feeling that warm little body in his arms, loved knowing she was totally dependent on him. It was Betsy who had pulled him out of his bout of bitterness and hate for Elizabeth.

It would always be Betsy who kept him on the straight and narrow, working to make his ranch successful. She deserved the best.

If they had a good crop of bull calves this season, he could escape some of the crippling debt Elizabeth had saddled him with. He'd been so in love with her he'd provided more than he should have, more than he could afford. But he'd wanted to make Elizabeth happy.

In return, she'd made him miserable and deeply in debt.

As he stared at the television in the family room with the others, he gritted his teeth. He was never going to let a woman do that to him again.

"John?"

His head snapped up. Debra was standing at the end of the couch, staring at him. "What?"

"May I speak to you for a moment?"

With the others, especially Bill, around him, he had no choice but to acquiesce.

Following Debra into the kitchen—a completely clean kitchen, he realized—he prepared himself for her demands. "What do you want?"

"I need a few things from the grocery store. Is there a car I can borrow, and do you have an account at the store or will you give me money?"

"I should've known. The kitchen is full of food! You haven't been here twenty-four hours and already you're demanding money!"

He expected her to try flirting to get her way, followed by crying. That was the pattern his first wife had used many times.

Instead, after staring at him for several seconds, she simply left the room.

After a moment, he followed her, sure she was going to plead her case with her uncle.

But when he entered the family room, there was no sign of her. "Did Debra come through here?" he asked.

Bill looked up in surprise. "She said good-night and went upstairs."

John was stunned. Why hadn't she pressed him? Come to think of it, Elizabeth had never asked for groceries. Her requests had always been personal. Was the kitchen missing some key ingredient Debra needed?

After pacing the room for several minutes, ignored by his men, he decided to go upstairs and find her. That was probably her plan, anyway.

The hallway was dark, but he saw a light shining under one door. That must be the bedroom she'd chosen for her own. He rapped on the door.

A soft voice answered, "Who is it?"

"It's John."

After a hesitation that irritated him, she opened the door about an inch. "I'm getting ready for bed, John. What do you want?"

"What did you want at the grocery store?"

She sighed. "I wanted to get some baby cereal and some chocolate chips for making cookies."

"Baby cereal? Why do you want baby cereal?"

"I'm guessing Betsy is at least nine months old. She should be eating cereal in the morning and adding solid foods during her meals. It will mean she'll sleep through the night."

"She will? Are you sure?"

"Yes. Haven't you taken her to the doctor for her checkups?"

"She went while Elizabeth— She went early on, but I didn't see any need. She's healthy!"

"Yes, I know. But he would've advised you about her feedings, if you had."

"So you mean baby food? Those little bottles?"

"Well, I can make a few things. I wasn't going to ask for too much at once. I wanted the chocolate chips to make cookies for Andy and to put in your lunches."

John put up his hand to stop her. "The car's in the garage. The key is on one of the hooks by the door. Sign the receipt at the general store and Charlie will put it on my account." He turned away and walked down the hall to the stairs.

So she really wanted groceries…. She was probably starting out slowly, hoping to lull him into acceptance, said a warning voice inside his head. Not Elizabeth's style, but you couldn't trust a woman. Any woman.

No one was late for breakfast the next morning. Maybe they were encouraged by visions of fluffy scrambled eggs, bacon, sausage and hot biscuits with jam that she'd found in the pantry, along with hot coffee.

Debra had gotten up at five-fifteen so she'd been

able to make their lunches, too. The bags were all ready, sitting on the kitchen cabinet for them when they finished their breakfast. Of course, since March in Wyoming was cold, their lunches wouldn't be warm, but they would be filling. She was proud of the food she'd provided. She couldn't imagine going all day, working as hard as these men did, without lunch.

"This is great, Debra," Bill said with a big smile. "Especially the hot biscuits."

"I'm glad you like everything, Uncle Bill."

Jess and Mikey paused, then Mikey asked, "He really is your uncle?"

"Yes, of course," Debra replied while her uncle protested. "Why wouldn't you believe that I'm Bill's niece?"

"Well," Jess said with a wink, "'cause you're lots prettier than him and you cook tons better."

Everyone but John laughed.

"Thank you for the compliments, but everyone has talents in different areas. Otherwise, life would be very dull."

As they filed out of the kitchen, Debra handed each of them his lunch. John was the last to leave and he didn't even pause. "No, thank you."

"You might as well take it since I've already made it for you." She held out the bag.

He glowered and hesitated. She held her breath, hoping he'd take it. Somehow it seemed important to her, as if his taking the lunch would be an act of approval.

"I don't have time for lunch," he muttered, and walked out of the house.

Debra stood there, tears forming in her eyes. She hadn't expected her new life to be easy, had she? Of course not. The best thing she could do was her job. Keep the house clean, cook and take care of Betsy, as well as Andy.

And not expect anything else. Especially not a husband.

She put the load of clothes in the dryer and then went upstairs to wake Andy. "Honey, it's time to get up and come eat breakfast."

"I want to stay in bed," Andy protested. "Eileen let me stay in bed as long as I wanted."

Which explained why she'd always had trouble getting him to bed in the evenings, she thought. She'd always assumed her son required less sleep. But, as usual, her mother had chosen the easiest path.

"There's no Eileen here, my dear. I'll put your clothes out while you go wash your face. Get dressed and come to the kitchen. I'll have breakfast ready."

She gently propelled her son into the bathroom. After she laid out his clothes, she went into Betsy's room. The baby was just stirring, stretching and yawning.

"Good morning, angel. Did you sleep well? First, I'll change your diaper, then we'll have breakfast. After that, you get a bath. If you're not too modest, I'll let Andy help. Then we'll go grocery shopping. How does that sound?"

As if she approved, Betsy smiled at her. Her whole face lit up and her eyes gleamed. She had the same eyes as her father, sea-blue, only his never sparkled in a smile.

Debra shrugged her shoulders and changed Betsy's diaper. Time to get things done, not think about John.

"How was Betsy this morning?" Bill asked John as they rode out a short time later.

John jerked back on his reins, startling his horse. Staring at Bill, he frantically searched his brain. "She—she didn't wake me up! Damn, she's probably sick or something. I've got to go back. I'll catch up with you!" he called over his shoulder as he urged his horse back toward the barn. All the way, he was telling himself he was the worst daddy in the world to leave his child without being sure she was all right.

He rode right up to the back door of the house and tied his horse to the limb of a tree nearby.

Opening the back door, he ran into the kitchen where he heard voices. There he found his baby daughter sitting in a high chair, babbling away and banging her fist on the tray.

"Just a minute, sweetie," Debra called over her shoulder. She set a plate of scrambled eggs on the table in front of Andy and gave Betsy a bottle.

Andy leaned forward and whispered something John couldn't hear, but he gathered the little boy mentioned his presence because Debra's gaze flew to him. "John? Is something wrong?"

As if hearing his name alerted Betsy, she began cooing and waving her arms. "I think your daughter is trying to say hello."

John crossed to the high chair. "Hello, Betsy. Did you miss Daddy?" He picked her up and kissed her cheek.

"Um, she hasn't had her bath yet, so she may not smell too good. I thought it best to bathe her after breakfast."

"That's fine. But she didn't wake me up at 4:00 a.m. as usual. I was afraid something was wrong."

"Oh, I'm sorry. I thought I told you. Solid food stays with the baby longer and helps her to sleep through the night."

"That's really all it took? I didn't believe— What did you feed her?"

"Last night I fed her some whipped potatoes."

"She might've choked on that!" John exclaimed.

"The spoonfuls were very small, John. I've fed a baby before."

"Yeah, but—"

"If you want me to wait until I take her to the doctor, I will. It's your choice."

"No, I guess— When are you going to the grocery store?"

"After breakfast and Betsy's bath. I didn't think he'd open before eight o'clock."

"Her baby seat is in the car. Make sure you strap her

in." He settled his daughter in her high chair again. "Be careful. Don't drive too fast."

"No, I won't."

He stared at her. "Am I acting like an idiot?"

"Just a little bit," Debra said with a smile. His obvious love for his child was very attractive and made it easy to forgive his difficult behavior toward her.

"Fine. Just—just get her home safely."

"I will, I promise."

John remounted and joined his crew, but his worries continued to dominate his thoughts. It was the first time someone else had taken Betsy anywhere.

Debra was unusually nervous when she drove the Cadillac Escalade to Westlake's general store. She'd never been in such an expensive vehicle. It seemed foolish to Debra to pay for such a costly truck just to be sure Betsy was safe.

It appeared the store owner agreed with her. "I couldn't believe when John ordered this here car for his wife," Charlie said. "Man, these things cost a fortune."

"Yes, so I've heard. But I guess it's water under the bridge."

"I don't know about that. He could sure sell it and pay off some debts."

"Would he get a lot for it?"

"Sure. He's hardly driven it since his wife died."

"Maybe he'll decide to do that. Thanks for your help with the groceries."

"Glad to do it. You've got your hands full with two little ones. Did you get everything you need?"

"I think so. Whatever Mrs. Richey did, she certainly organized and stocked the kitchen well."

"Shoot, that wasn't Mrs. Richey. John had a housekeeper after he got married. Mrs. Richey insisted. But she left just before Mrs. Richey died. The lady of the house was unhappy with her work and fired her. Just as well. John couldn't afford her salary with all the debt he'd incurred, anyway."

"I hope she found another job."

"Sure she did. A good cook can always find a job."

"I'm glad to hear it. Thanks again for your help."

Debra had a lot to think about as she drove home. Why hadn't John sold the Escalade? His wife wasn't here to use it. She certainly didn't need it. She could drive John's or Bill's truck whenever she needed to go to town.

This trip to town was certainly productive, she thought as she eyed the big box in the back. John wouldn't be upset that she'd bought Betsy a playpen, would he? After all, the baby could already pull herself up and would learn to walk if she had a safe place to try.

She could crawl around on the rug in the family room if someone was in there with her, but if Debra was to complete all her chores, she couldn't watch the baby every minute. And Andy was too young for that responsibility. But he could watch *Sesame Street* and keep Betsy company if she was in the playpen.

As soon as they got home, Debra sat on the floor, with Betsy right beside her, and put together the playpen. Andy thought he was helping when he handed his mother the screws. It may have slowed down the process a little, but she believed in building a child's self-esteem, even if it took a little lie now and then.

Soon she had Betsy in the new playpen and Andy on the sofa watching the television. She did chores until it was time to fix lunch, which reminded her that John hadn't taken a sandwich like the other men. He would be starving. She planned her evening menu accordingly.

Both kids went down for a nap in the afternoon and she cleaned the big, beautiful house. Then she did some baking after they woke up. Andy loved baking cookies with her. Truth be told, she probably enjoyed it more than he did. Even Betsy was enthusiastic, joining in their laughter. While the cookies baked, Debra sat and spoke to the baby, helping her make sounds and try to make words.

The easiest one was Da-da. Debra wasn't sure the baby knew she was naming her father, but she thought it would be fun for John. She could clearly remember the first time Andy called her Ma-ma.

Andy sat down for a cookie as soon as it cooled, the chocolate chips soft and gooey. She enjoyed a cookie, too, but more than that she relished this precious time with her son. If she'd been back in Kansas City, she'd just be getting home from the diner and no doubt be exhausted and looking forward to bed.

"Why can't Betsy have a cookie, Mommy?" Andy asked, breaking into her thoughts.

"Because chocolate isn't good for babies, Andy. She'll have to grow more teeth before she can eat chips, anyway."

"But I like them!" Andy said.

"I know, honey. Betsy will, too, when she gets a little older. Oh, I need to feed the two of you so you can have your bath and go to bed before the men come in."

"Why don't I get to stay up and see the cowboys?"

"You will, honey, but right now they're getting in late, too late for you to eat your dinner. After calving season, you'll see a lot of them."

"What's calving season?"

"That's when the mama cows have their babies." When her son opened his mouth to ask more questions, she hurriedly said, "No, no more questions. I have too much to do right now."

Once the children were in bed, she began preparing dinner, trying to fix dishes she thought John would like. Which was hard to do since she didn't know any of his likes or dislikes.

Why did she keep thinking about the man?

He was driving her crazy.

She couldn't possibly be attracted to him, could she? Well, she was sympathetic. She understood the anger he felt toward his first wife. She'd felt some anger toward her first husband, such as he was. But she wasn't going to be hurt now. She was going to concentrate on her job and the children.

And one angry man.

CHAPTER THREE

"BETSY'S upstairs asleep, again?" John demanded fiercely when he came in for dinner that evening.

"Yes," Debra said and followed him out of the kitchen. "John, I thought a regular schedule would be beneficial both for Andy and—"

"I'm not talking about Andy! I care about Betsy. I want to see *her* when I get home at night!"

Debra stopped short in the hall. "Well," she said, her tone terse, "I guess that's just another lie." She turned back toward the kitchen.

"What are you talking about?"

"Uncle Bill said you'd be a daddy for Andy."

Damn. Even he wouldn't be mean to a kid. Didn't she know that about him, at least? He was just in a snit—at Debra, mostly—and disappointed that even though the ranch work was getting done now, he was seeing less and less of his daughter. From the look on Debra's face, he knew her feelings had gotten hurt. He knew he needed to apologize. Shoot, he was never any good at saying sorry. Often enough he'd had to eat crow when Elizabeth was upset—whether it was his fault or not. But it was not a skill he'd ever really acquired. He was about to give it a try when Debra shot him a narrowed glance as sharp as a new blade and walked away.

He'd apologize later. Seeing Betsy was important now.

Upstairs, John found his baby sleeping peacefully. He touched her downy hair and patted her back, but after several minutes, he realized she wasn't going to awaken. Satisfying himself with a kiss on her cheek, he went back downstairs and showered. Everyone was already eating.

"Sorry, John," Bill told him, a worried look on his face. "Debra told us to go ahead and eat."

"No problem. I just wanted to check on Betsy." The other two men welcomed him, but he noticed Debra said nothing as she passed the food to him. She'd get over her anger when he apologized later, not in front of the men, of course.

He waited until after they'd all finished eating, including the apple pie she put on the table. He'd never tasted better. But he thought his men had praised her enough.

Trying to wait out his men, he sat at the table, not moving as she stacked the dishes.

"Did you need something else, Mr. Richey?"

Her formality surprised him. "Why are you calling me that?"

"Is that not your name?" she asked coolly.

He ignored her question. "I was going to apologize—"

"Not necessary. You made everything clear." She began loading the dishwasher.

Why did women make it so hard to say sorry? he thought to himself.

"Debra, stop! I want to apologize to you."

"I'm sorry, but I have a lot of chores and I'm tired."

"You're not some damned Cinderella, Debra."

"No, of course not. I'm your housekeeper."

"You're my wife!"

"You and I both know that isn't true. If you'll excuse me, I need to start a load of clothes." She left the dishes and walked out of the room.

He followed her. "I'll be able to hire a housekeeper in the fall."

She whirled around and glared at him. When she started back down to the laundry room, John didn't follow.

What did he say? He'd tried apologizing, he'd tried giving her a break—and whatever he'd said only made her angrier. Why would she be unhappy about him hiring a housekeeper? Elizabeth had insisted on it.

And why did she call him Mr. Richey? They were married. He may have been slow warming up to it but he'd still stood in front of the reverend and exchanged vows, hadn't he? Didn't that count for anything?

John went back to the kitchen for another cup of coffee.

She'd unsettled him so much he figured on being up half the night, anyway. One thing he was certain of—Debra may make him crazy, but neither she nor her so-called schedule was going to keep him from seeing his daughter.

Tomorrow he'd come in early.

Debra stopped her uncle before he could leave. "May I talk to you a minute, Uncle Bill?"

"Look, honey, I know he's not being a good husband right now, but he'll get better."

She put up a hand to stop him. "I don't want to discuss John with you, at least not as my husband. I drove the Escalade to the general store today. Charlie said John could make a lot of money if he sold it. I wondered why he hadn't. Surely the money would be helpful for the ranch. He could even hire another cowboy to help out."

Bill stared at her. "You mean that?"

"Mean what?"

"You're not asking for something for yourself? You would understand if he spent it on the ranch?"

"The car doesn't belong to me. And I can as easily drive your truck into town if I need to, can't I?"

"You sure can. This is great, Debra. I can't wait to tell John what you said."

"No! You are not to mention me at all. You had this idea on your own."

"But, Debra—"

"No, Uncle Bill. You owe me that much." If John

decided to hire the housekeeper now instead of in the fall, well, that was life. She and Andy would find somewhere to go. After all, hadn't Charlie said a good cook could always find a job? She felt her stomach clench at the thought. But she couldn't possibly have already built an attachment to the ranch…or the man…. Could she?

Guilt had overcome Bill. He put an arm around her. "Yeah, honey, I do owe you. Okay, I won't say anything about you, but he should know you thought up the idea and didn't want to profit from it."

"No. It won't matter."

Bill tried to argue with her, but Debra held up her hand. "I'm tired, and I'm going up to bed."

"Okay, honey. Thanks again."

After she had left the mudroom, Bill stood there, trying to figure out what to do. He decided to tell John he came up with the idea overnight. John would be too suspicious if he went back in to tell him now. And he'd promised Debra.

He felt like a dummy for not making that suggestion himself. John and he had both been in a fog after Elizabeth's betrayal and death. He guessed they hadn't been thinking too clearly. He only hoped John would agree with the decision.

When John came to breakfast the next morning, he was surprised to find his baby daughter in her high chair. "Good morning, sweetheart," he said immediately.

Mikey and Jess were already at the table. Mikey said, "Aw, you don't have to sweet talk Debra. She's already cooked breakfast."

Debra said nothing and kept her back to him.

"I was talking to Betsy," John hurriedly said. "She hasn't been joining us for breakfast since, uh, since Debra came."

Debra turned around and hurriedly put a plate of scrambled eggs on the table. "You should feed Betsy her cereal. Just be sure to give her small spoonfuls."

Then she turned back to the kitchen counter.

"Did you get up on the wrong side of the bed, Debra?" Mikey asked. "Oh, maybe I should ask John that question," he added with a chuckle.

Debra turned on the water at the sink, ignoring them.

Bill came rushing in. "Sorry I'm late." No one even looked at him. "What's wrong?"

"Uh, nothing," Mikey said. Then he bent over and whispered, "I think they had a fight."

Bill looked at John. He leaned closer to him. "Did you and Debra have a fight?"

"No. Why—" Betsy chose that moment to grab the spoon and dump its contents on her tray and herself. "Betsy, no!"

"Perhaps I should feed her while you eat your breakfast," Debra said quietly.

"No, I'll feed my daughter."

Without saying anything, Debra moved away. The

lunches were on the cabinet and as the other men filed out, Debra handed them each a bag. They thanked her warmly.

She stood there watching John trying to get some cereal down his daughter. But she didn't bother offering to feed Betsy again. After several minutes, John looked up. "I can't seem to get much in her mouth."

"I'll finish feeding her, if you want."

"Thanks."

He grabbed his hat and hurried out without adding that he wanted to see his daughter at dinner that evening. During his sleepless night he'd come to realize that long a day might be difficult for Betsy. But he was glad Debra had realized what he wanted, seeing his daughter at breakfast.

Maybe things would work out, after all.

Betsy protested as her daddy left the room. Debra hurried over to console the baby and help her drink her milk. It was in a Tommy Tippie cup rather than a bottle. "It's okay, Betsy. He'll get better with practice. Now, let me feed you some cereal before it gets cold."

After she'd fed Betsy and changed her diaper, she woke up Andy and fed him breakfast. Then she put in a load of clothes while the dishwasher went through its cycles.

She was surprised when the phone rang midmorning.

Hesitantly, she lifted the receiver. "Hello?"

"Hello? Is this the housekeeper?"

"Uh, yes."

"Oh, good. I wasn't sure you still worked there. It's

Adele from Westlake Auxiliary. We're having our annual fair again this year. It's an opportunity to sell things you don't want or things you've made to sell, like jam, quilts, things like that. I hope you'll be able to bring something. Ten percent of whatever you sell goes to the Auxiliary. We're trying to buy a new fire truck, you know."

Debra didn't know.

"When is it, Adele?"

"In a month, April 12. I know I shouldn't ask, but I hope your boss will let you bring some of Elizabeth's things. I wasn't a big fan of hers, but she had fabulous taste."

"I'll certainly ask."

"Oh, good. Just report to Mrs. Jones before eight o'clock."

"I don't know Mrs. Jones," Debra said quickly before the woman could hang up.

"Just ask around. Everyone knows her." Click. The line went dead.

But it left Debra with a lot of questions and a few plans. First, she went into the master bedroom and found the lady's closet. Why had John kept the clothes in the closet? Was it the same reason he had kept the car? Was he too depressed or too busy to make changes? Or did he still care for his first wife in spite of how she'd treated him?

Debra knew enough to recognize some designer names among the clothes that filled the closet. She figured John could make an attractive sum of money by selling his wife's belongings. But she knew instinctively he wouldn't do that. He was too proud.

Then she wondered what she could make to sell at the fair. Quilts were the best option. Her grandmother had taught her how to make quilts as a young girl. After her grandmother died, her mother refused to allow her to continue to quilt. She said it made too much of a mess.

She'd need a sewing machine. She decided to check all the closets before she worried about buying one. In a hall closet, her search paid off. She found an almost new sewing machine, along with a bag of scrap material, almost as if someone had quilted in the house before. Delighted with her find, she carried the machine and the material to the kitchen.

Her spirits lifted. A good thing, too, because they'd been pretty low.

"What's that, Mommy?" Andy had followed her.

"It's a sewing machine."

"What's it do?"

Debra couldn't help but smile. "I make things with it. And I can repair holes in your clothes with it."

"Can I make it do something?"

"Not yet. When you're older, you can if you want. Mostly ladies do it." Debra drew a deep breath. "I think *Sesame Street* is on. Do you want to watch it?"

"Oh, yeah!"

She fixed him a plate of cookies and a glass of milk and turned on the television. Then Betsy called from upstairs.

Debra had hoped the baby would nap longer. She wanted some time with the sewing machine. But she'd find the time, somehow.

By the end of the day, she'd made a plan for the quilt she was going to make. Whatever she could get done before the fair, she would sell and put the money away so she'd have something to live off of once John got his housekeeper.

She let Betsy sleep a longer time that afternoon. Then she got her up and dressed her to have dinner with her father. Andy, who had stayed up most of the afternoon, ate his dinner early and got bathed. Then she tucked her son into his bed, read him a story from his favorite book and kissed him good-night.

She put a barrette in Betsy's soft curls to keep them out of the way.

"Okay, little girl. You look very pretty for your daddy. Now I'm going to put you in your playpen while I finish up dinner."

Betsy held up her arms, calling, "Ma-ma." Debra tried to ignore her, but she couldn't. "Okay, how about I put you in your high chair for when Daddy comes in." Immediately the baby switched to "Da-da," her gaze fastened on the door.

Just as Debra had dinner on the table, she heard the men come in. The men, except for John, were now showering in the bunkhouse, since they all had a supply of clean clothes to choose from. They were coming in clean to dinner, now.

But where was John?

As soon as her uncle Bill came into the kitchen, Debra asked, "Where's John?"

"Didn't he stop by the house? He said he'd let you know that he'd be late to dinner."

With all three men staring at her, Debra lied. "Oh, yes, I forgot."

She filled a plate and covered it with plastic wrap. "Can I get you anything else?" she asked the others.

"Aren't you going to eat, honey?" Bill asked.

Surprised, Debra looked up. "I'll eat later. Right now I need to feed Betsy."

She fed the baby girl as she babbled at Debra. Several times she said, "Da-da," and the men looked up.

"Is she calling her daddy?" Jess asked.

"I think so. I'm hoping he'll be pleased."

"Are you going to mind cooking for another cowboy?" Mikey asked, a frown on his face.

"Another cowboy?" Debra asked, surprised.

"Yeah, the boss is hiring another cowboy." Jess stared at her. "We can start doing our own cooking if we need to."

"Don't be silly, Jess. It's as easy to cook for five as it is four. It won't be a problem. It's my job."

They all heard the rumble of a big engine. Debra

looked out the kitchen window and saw the Escalade pull in by the window. Before she could say anything, they heard a car door close and the Escalade leave.

Debra stared at the door just as it opened and John came into the kitchen. "Sorry I'm late," he said with a glance at her.

She reheated his plate and put it in front of John.

Turning to Betsy, she prompted, "Betsy, did you say hello to Daddy?"

Betsy began waving her arms and chanting, "Da-da."

John, who had just picked up a fork, stopped in midaction and stared at his baby. "She—she's saying Daddy?"

"Yes, I believe so," Debra said in an offhand manner.

All the men began talking to Betsy, praising her and prompting her to say more, and she suddenly stopped talking, staring at each of them.

Debra consoled the baby. "I think your enthusiasm has frightened Betsy," she told the men.

They fell silent. "Betsy, did you say hi to Daddy?" Debra repeated and watched the child start babbling again.

Debra pulled out a chair next to Betsy. "I'll feed her while you eat, if you don't mind." She wasn't sure about John's reaction.

"Aren't you going to eat?" John asked.

"I've already eaten," she lied, and began feeding Betsy the rest of her dinner.

"Where's Andy?" John asked suddenly.

Surprised, Debra said, "He's in bed."

"We haven't seen him since you first got here." Jess looked puzzled.

"It's not good for him to wait this late to eat."

"So you're cooking two dinners each day?" Bill asked.

Debra avoided anyone's prying eyes. "It's no big deal."

"Shouldn't Andy be eating with us?" John asked.

"No, I don't think so." She wasn't going to let her son fall in love with the home she'd found for them when she knew now it was only temporary. That would lead to heartbreak.

"I think I should get to know Andy." She heard the stubbornness in John's voice.

"We'll discuss it later, John."

"Hey, guys, pillow talk!" Mikey proclaimed with enthusiasm.

"Would you like more gravy and potatoes, Mikey?" Debra asked, knowing food would distract the young man.

"Oh, yeah, if you've got some more. I'm really hungry this evening."

Jess slapped his friend on the back. "You're always hungry, Mikey."

"Hey, I'm still a growing boy!"

"You eat any more and John will have to add a surcharge for food," Jess teased.

Debra breathed a sigh of relief that she had escaped the questions. Until she caught John's stare. His blue eyes bore into her. Though she shivered, she continued to ignore him. It wasn't easy. He seemed to dominate a room every time he entered.

How was she going to distract him?

"Did you hire another cowboy?" she tried.

John stiffened. "How do you know that?"

"The others mentioned it." She returned his stare. "Were you going to wait and let him just show up one morning to surprise me?"

"No, I wasn't. I was going to discuss the changes in the household when we were alone."

"I think I've already worked things out except for the date. When will he be here?"

"He's moving into the bunkhouse tonight. He'll be here for breakfast in the morning."

"Fine. I'll increase what I cook."

"I don't really think you need to, Debra," Jess said. "We could all use a little less breakfast now that we're getting lunches, too." Jess gave her a rueful smile.

"Hey!" Mikey protested. "Speak for yourself."

"This is not up for discussion!" John shouted.

Debra didn't even flinch, but the men were surprised. "Yes, boss," Jess said. "Uh, thanks for the dinner, Debra." He left the table followed quickly by his pal, Mikey.

"John, why are you yelling at everyone?" Bill asked.

"I'm trying to have a conversation with my wife, but everyone seems to think he has the right to interfere." John glared at Bill.

"Are you talking about me?" Bill asked in outrage.

"I'm the ranch manager. I'm supposed to know what's going on."

John blew out the hot air that seemed to be building in him. "I didn't mean—I thought I should tell Debra in private since I sold the truck she was supposed to have at her disposal."

"Hell, man, it was her idea!" Bill said. Debra saw when the realization hit Bill and he knew he'd blown his promise.

She continued to feed Betsy, ignoring the two men, pretending she hadn't heard Bill's statement

"What do you mean it was her idea?" John asked.

"I lied to you, because she asked me to. She didn't think you'd accept such a good idea from her. But I think she should get the credit for it."

John stared at her. "This was your idea?"

Debra stiffened her back. "Yes."

"Why?"

"I thought you could use the extra help for the calving season."

"I don't need you to take pity on me!"

"So now you're going to cut off your nose to spite your face?" she asked unemotionally.

"No, damn you, I'm not. The new cowboy will be here tomorrow for breakfast. Be prepared!" He got up to stride out of the room, but Betsy stopped him. "Da-da!"

Debra watched as Betsy caused her daddy to melt all over himself, moving to the high chair to lift her out of it. "Sorry, baby, Daddy forgot." He cuddled her against him.

"I think I should take—" Debra began, having recognized a pattern in Betsy's behavior after a big meal.

"No! She's my child. I can take care of her."

"Of course," she said. But she watched out of the corner of her eye as Betsy performed as expected. John wrinkled his nose as a distinct odor rose from Betsy's diaper.

CHAPTER FOUR

DEBRA looked at John, but she didn't say anything.

"I'll take care of her," he repeated and carried his baby daughter out of the kitchen, heading for the stairs and Betsy's bedroom.

Debra's husband had died before Andy was born, but she'd heard the waitresses at Joe's Diner complaining about their husbands refusing to deal with dirty diapers. John certainly wasn't like them. She admired that about him.

She cleaned the kitchen, as she usually did, not wanting to start the day behind. Especially in the morning with another mouth to feed. Thinking about the laundry, she decided she should organize the men, having one of them bring his dirty laundry each day, so she could control the amount of clothes she had to wash. Since she was going to begin the quilt the next day, she needed to organize her time.

The men, minus John, of course, were in the family

room watching television. She waited for a commercial to explain her plan, assigning each of them a laundry day.

Once that was done, she turned around to find John staring at her, clearly irritated by something. That wasn't a big surprise. He seemed to always be upset about something. "Is there a problem, John? Did Betsy—"

"Betsy did just fine!" When Bill turned to look at him, John gestured to the kitchen.

Whatever was bothering him couldn't be discussed in earshot of the men, she figured. Reluctantly she preceded him into the kitchen, then turned around and said, "Well?"

"You cleaned my bedroom!"

"So?"

"I thought I told you not to go in there!"

"You can be sure I won't when you're in there, if that's what you're afraid of."

"I'm not afraid! I just want my privacy!"

"I'm the housekeeper. I'm not going to have my reputation ruined because you like to live in filth. Your bathroom hadn't been cleaned in months!"

"I don't think your reputation as a housekeeper will suffer. And you have enough to do with the two kids and the laundry and cooking."

"Fine!"

"Fine!" He left the kitchen.

Debra got out the sewing machine and began work on the quilt, taking her frustration out in a positive way. Eventually she calmed down to think rationally. As long as she continued to clean his room, he wouldn't notice the change anymore. Well, he might if she made his bed. She'd made his bed with clean sheets today and she thought he'd sleep better. But, of course, he'd never admit it.

Bill came in to tell her good-night. When he found her sewing, he wanted to know what she was doing.

"I'm quilting, Uncle Bill. I used to do this with Grandma."

"Hey, you're right. I have a quilt my mom sent to me. I'd forgotten where I'd gotten it. Who is this one for?"

"The Westlake Auxiliary's fair. This way I can make some money for the future."

"Honey, John will give you money. You're working hard enough for it."

"No, I don't want his money. I'll make my own. Good night, Uncle Bill."

She'd thought about asking Uncle Bill to promise not to tell John about her plan, but his promising hadn't worked out so well last time. So she decided not to emphasize her secret. She'd just let it go and with any luck her uncle would forget it.

When John returned to the kitchen a few minutes later, Debra sighed. The children were less of a problem than the adults.

"What are you doing?"

"I'm quilting."

"We don't need any quilts."

"John, I've done the cooking and the laundry, the house is clean and the children are asleep. If there's anything you need me to do, I'll do it. Otherwise, I'll do what I like to do, which is quilting. Okay?" Her tone was harsh but she had to stand up for herself.

"I wasn't criticizing you, Debra."

"Good." She started the sewing machine again.

He stood there looking at her, and she could feel his eyes boring into her as she sewed. When he finally left the kitchen, without saying anything else, she breathed a sigh of relief.

The next morning after breakfast and the introduction of the new cowboy, Darrell, Bill and John rode out together.

"Good breakfast this morning. I sure do love pancakes," Bill said.

"Yeah, but didn't you think Debra looked pale?" John asked.

Bill looked at his boss cautiously. "Are you complaining about breakfast?"

"Hell no! It was great. But Debra didn't seem as—as vibrant as she usually does."

"Maybe she stayed up too late last night working on that quilt."

"Yeah, maybe so," John agreed. After a moment, he said, "I noticed you brought a big bag of laundry in this morning. You trying to make her work extra hard?"

"No, didn't you hear? Oh, I guess you were upstairs

with Betsy. Debra assigned each of us a day to bring in all our laundry. It saves her sorting everything and it keeps her laundry load kind of even. I thought it was pretty smart of her."

"Yeah, I guess so. When is my day?"

"John, you're her husband and the boss. You can have something washed whenever you want it."

"She cleaned my room yesterday," John abruptly said.

"Good."

"I told her not to do it again."

"Are you crazy, man? She's *supposed* to clean your room! It's one of the perks of being married!"

"I can take care of it myself."

"Oh, so you don't do enough in the saddle all day?"

"Yeah, but—"

"You're cutting off your nose to spite your face!" Bill shouted.

"That's what Debra said, too."

"So? She's right. That's an expression my mother used to use a lot. And she was right, too. You're not giving Debra a chance. She's doing everything you asked her to do and you're still complaining."

John hung his head. Bill was right. He had to admit that. Debra had far exceeded his expectations. She worked hard and cooked well. She was great with Betsy. She hadn't asked for anything. Elizabeth had demanded so much he'd almost gone bankrupt.

So why was he complaining?

Because he was afraid to get close to another woman, to make himself vulnerable.

He didn't like admitting that. He'd always believed he could face down anyone or anything. But he couldn't.

Not a woman.

After only four days in her new life, Debra had a set routine. It made everything much easier. And having an entire day to do her work was wonderful. She would admit to herself that her life was much better here in Wyoming than it had been in Kansas.

When John hired a housekeeper and didn't want her anymore, she might look for a housekeeper position somewhere in Wyoming. Maybe even close enough to come visit Betsy.

It would be difficult to leave Betsy. And John? She had to admit an attraction she hadn't wanted to feel. Sure, he was a good-looking man, tall, with solid muscles and handsome features, but more than all that, she liked the way his eyes crinkled when he smiled. If they could start over, have a normal marriage, she thought she might be happier than she'd ever been before.

That thought brought a warm blush to her cheeks. Thinking about being in John's arms, feeling his touch, was something she shouldn't be thinking about. It didn't seem to be part of their marriage agreement.

And it shouldn't be since he was going to get rid of

her in the fall. So she only had about six months of married life left.

She took some time that afternoon to play with Betsy and Andy on the rug in the den. Andy was teaching the baby to crawl. Betsy was a fast learner.

"Very good, Betsy," Debra praised. She picked up the baby and gave her a kiss on the cheek. "You're a very good crawler."

Betsy squealed and said, "Ma-ma!"

"Yes, sweetheart, but I don't think your daddy will like that word."

"Why not, Mommy?" Andy asked. "You said Betsy was my sister. That makes you her mommy."

"I know, honey, but John doesn't quite believe that."

"Didn't you get married?"

Debra didn't want to answer that question, but, unfortunately for her, her son was a little too smart for her own good. "Yes, we did, but…well, it takes time to adjust to the change, honey." Trying to change the subject, she pointed at Betsy. "Oh, look, she's pulling herself up. Pretty soon she'll be walking."

"I can teach her," Andy exclaimed.

"Not yet. She still needs to crawl. Can you give her another example of crawling?"

"Sure!" Andy agreed, getting on his hands and knees to lead Betsy across the rug. Betsy fell right in behind him and crawled just like he did.

A few minutes later, Debra put Betsy in her playpen.

"I have to go fix your supper, Andy. You watch *Sesame Street* and Betsy will watch from here."

"I want to have supper with everyone else, like Betsy does. Why can't I, Mommy?"

Debra sighed. She'd been afraid Andy would complain about his early bedtime. "Sweetie, I just think it's better this way."

"Please, Mommy?"

Debra finally relented. "Okay, we'll try it for tonight. If you get too tired, you'll have to start going to bed early."

"I promise, Mommy!" Andy gave her a hug. "Will I get to sit by John?"

"I think you'll sit between me and Uncle Bill."

"But I want—"

"Andy!"

"Yes, Mommy," he said, giving up his request. He turned obediently to the TV and Debra headed to the kitchen.

She had dinner almost ready when she heard an engine start up out back. She stepped to the window and saw Bill driving away in his truck.

Debra didn't know what could make Bill leave right before dinner. She hoped nothing was wrong. Maybe she could ask John when he got there.

When she heard the back door open, she hurried to the kitchen door, eager to find out what was going on. But it wasn't John who walked through the door. It was Mikey, Jess and Darrell.

"Where are John and Bill?" she asked.

"Uh, don't get upset, Debra," Mikey said.

"About what?"

Jess stepped forward. "John fell off his horse."

"John? What happened?"

"His horse was surprised by a snake."

"Is he hurt?"

Jess nodded, watching her closely, as if he feared she'd burst into tears. "We think he broke his leg, that's all. Mikey made it sound worse than it was."

"So Bill took him to the doctor?"

"That's right. They should be back soon."

"Thanks, Jess. And you, too, Mikey." She forced a smile. "Come on in. I've got dinner ready." She worked hard at sounding normal, but all she could think about was John suffering. Truth be told, she did feel like bursting into tears, as they'd expected. But she wouldn't. "How was your first day, Darrell?" she asked.

"Just fine, Mrs. Richey."

"Call me Debra. Excuse me a moment. I'll go get the children. They're both eating with us tonight."

She brought Andy into the room with Betsy in her other arm. "Gentlemen, this is my son, Andy. He's three years old, and he likes cowboys. And, of course, you all know Betsy."

The men greeted Andy who was still holding on to his mother.

"Sweetheart, why don't you sit over by Jess, next to Betsy's high chair."

Andy looked around. "Where's John? And Uncle Bill?"

The men glanced at Debra. "Uh," she stammered, "they had to run an errand." No sense upsetting the boy till she knew something.

As Andy got in the chair she'd indicated, she settled Betsy in her high chair. Then she began serving dinner. She kept looking at the window even as she fed Betsy.

"I'm sure Bill and the boss will be along soon," Jess said, having noticed her anxiety.

"I guess—" The ringing phone interrupted her. She jumped up at once to get it. "Hello?"

"Honey, it's Bill."

"How is John?"

"The boys told you, I guess. He's going to be okay, but he's broken his leg in several places. Doc says he's going to be down for a while. The thing is, they don't have the staff here to take care of him. Doc said if you can take care of him and keep him off his feet, he won't have to go away to a hospital. It'll only be for a couple of days. The leg is all swollen and they can't put him in a cast until the swelling goes down."

"Of course I can take care of him, Bill. Bring him home at once."

"You sure? He can be a bear when he's injured."

"Are you sure I'll notice the change?" she asked with

a grim smile. She felt guilty about that comment, but John had been difficult in the past.

Bill hesitated. "I guess not. Okay, we'll be there in about half an hour. Ask the guys to hang around so they can help carry him to his bed."

"Yes, I will."

After hanging up the phone, she turned and told the men of Bill's request. They immediately agreed.

"Will you keep an eye on Andy and Betsy for a minute? I need to go straighten up the bedroom before they get here."

Mikey agreed to try feeding Betsy.

Debra left the kitchen and ran down the hall for John's bedroom. She straightened the bed. She'd just changed the sheets yesterday. She didn't think he wore pajamas. At least, she hadn't washed any. She quickly searched through his drawers and found a lone pair in a bottom drawer. She laid them out on the bed, along with a T-shirt.

Then she hurried back to the table to take over feeding Betsy and supervising Andy. They had all just finished eating when they heard Bill's truck returning. The three men went out to assist him with John.

"Mommy, what happened to John?" Andy asked.

"He fell off his horse, sweetie, and broke his leg."

"Does it hurt?"

"Yes, a lot. Now, I need you to run upstairs and put on your pajamas. I'll be up to tuck you in as soon as I can."

"But I haven't had my bath, Mommy."

"I know, but we're going to skip it tonight. Okay? Now, I have to get Betsy in bed, too. Scoot along. Betsy and I will be right behind you."

She changed Betsy's diaper and put her in a nightgown and tucked her into bed. Fortunately, the baby was agreeable and settled down right away.

Debra ran into Andy's room and kissed her son goodnight. She told him to get in bed and she'd be up to see him later. Then she hurried down the stairs.

The men were just then carrying John toward his bedroom. She slipped ahead of them and turned down the covers. John was moaning and seemed to be under the influence of some drugs. He didn't even seem to realize that Debra was there.

"I thought it might be good if he put on the pajama bottoms and a T-shirt. Wouldn't he be more comfortable?" she asked.

"Probably," Bill said. "But he might start cussing if we tried that."

"I've heard cussing before, Uncle Bill."

"I don't think you should be in here," Bill whispered.

"Who do you think is going to take care of him during the day? You and the others are going to be out working your tails off, trying to cover for him."

"That's true. Okay. Try to move his leg as little as possible. The brace doesn't hold it all that steady."

"Do you need us for this, Bill?" Jess asked.

"Uh, naw, Debra and I will handle it. Thanks for the help." He said nothing else as the men filed out. Then he looked at Debra. "Hopefully they'll forget all this before John talks to them again."

"You're making a big deal about nothing. I'll pull the jeans down as you lift him off the bed. We need to do it quickly to minimize his pain."

"Okay. Let's do it." Bill leaned over his boss and slid his hands under him.

Debra unzipped his jeans and pulled them over his hips as quickly as she could. Then she carefully slid them down his legs. A groan told her she'd caused him some pain. But the jeans were now off. Then they slipped on the loose pajama bottoms.

"Maybe we should leave his shirt on him until he's awake and can help with the T-shirt," Bill suggested.

"Good idea. Where are his pain pills, and can he have more now?" Debra waited for Bill to dig the bottle out of his pocket. Then she read the directions. "Every four hours? I guess he took some before he left the doctor's office?"

"Yeah, about seven-thirty. So he can't have any more until eleven-thirty. You'll be asleep long before then. I'm sure he can wait for them first thing in the morning." Bill took a step toward the door. "You don't need me anymore, do you?"

"No, but I saved you some dinner if you want it. It's in the fridge."

"Thanks, honey. I'm starved."

Once she was left alone with John, she slipped two extra pillows under his leg to elevate it a little. Then she pulled the sheet and a blanket over his body. Before leaving the room, she turned out the light, hoping he would fall asleep.

She hurried upstairs to check on her son. The light was still on and the book she'd given him to look at had fallen to the floor. She gave him a gentle kiss as he slept and slipped out of his room, turning off the light as she went.

Then she checked on Betsy, who was sound asleep, also.

There were three children now, she thought. John was going to be as helpless as his daughter, and probably much grumpier. But now she would have a chance to get to know him. Only seeing him at meals meant she knew little about him. She had told herself that was a good thing, but she looked forward to understanding him a little better.

Determined to stay awake until eleven-thirty when she could give him more pain pills, she went down to the kitchen. First she cleaned up, then she got to work on the quilt.

Three hours later, she went to check on John, carrying a glass of water and two pills. He was groaning as he wriggled, trying to find a comfortable position.

She sat down on the side of the bed and put her

hand on his chest, feeling the steady thump of his heart. "John? John, wake up. I have more pain medicine for you."

"It hurts," he muttered.

"I know it does," she said soothingly. "If you can raise up on your elbows, I'll give you the pills and a glass of water. Come on, John."

She coaxed him into taking the pills, then sat beside him, soothing him until she saw the medicine take hold and relax him a bit. He was such a handsome man when he relaxed. Very lightly she touched his brow, then traced his jawline, strong and chiseled, down to his chin and up to his mouth. She lingered over his lips, firm and pink, and had to fight the urge to see what they tasted like.

As if she were a child reluctantly following an adult's directions, she got up and, with a sigh and a last glance at him, she shut off the light.

It was for the best, she thought as she dragged her feet to her own room. There was no sense in kissing her husband....

John knew it was still dark outside when he woke up, but he didn't care. He wanted relief from the pain he was feeling. He hadn't connected the pain to his leg, but he did when he tried to move it.

Almost at once he heard a soft voice telling him to raise up and take more pain pills. Without opening his eyes, he did as the voice suggested and swallowed the pills with the water. Then he fell back upon the pillow. A soft hand soothed his brow and he turned into the hand, liking the feel of it.

Slowly he lost consciousness again.

"Mommy, where are you taking that food?" Andy asked as he sat by the playpen amusing Betsy.

"Remember, last night at supper we talked about John having broken his leg? Well, he can't come to the kitchen to eat. I'm taking him some food."

"Can I help?"

"No, sweetie. Stay here and keep an eye on Betsy."

She reached the bedroom in time to hear John groaning. "John, I've brought you some breakfast," she announced in gentle tones. His eyes flew open and he stared at her as she put the tray on his bed.

"I need medicine," he muttered.

"I agree, but you also need to eat. I brought you a biscuit, some scrambled eggs and bacon and orange juice. Eat something and I'll give you your pain pills." She scooped up some scrambled eggs to entice him. She never expected him to open his mouth and let her bring the forkful to its destination. Was he even coherent? "Maybe I'd better put some more pillows behind you to help you sit up a little. Can you lean forward?"

John made the effort, but it wasn't an easy task. "I'm—I'm so weak."

"I think any accident takes a lot out of you," she

said soothingly as she helped him. "Now we can manage better."

She was about to continue feeding him when his hand reached out for the fork. When he was unable to do it on his own, she took over. An odd sensation nestled in her middle at taking care of him, seeing him so vulnerable. No doubt he'd hate it, but she actually enjoyed seeing him let down his defenses for a change. When he finished, she bent over him to remove the pillows from behind him so he could go back to sleep.

"You smell good," he mumbled.

Debra came to an abrupt halt. That was the first compliment he'd ever paid her, other than slight praise about her cooking. She stared at him, hoping he might say something that told her he knew who he was talking to. But he was already drifting to sleep.

With a sigh, she picked up the tray and headed back to the kitchen. She had some baking to do. The cookies disappeared fast around here.

John should be ready for more pain pills at about twelve-thirty. She could feed him some lunch and then give him the medicine and have the rest of the afternoon free.

But she feared she might spend more time thinking about the hunk she'd married than she should. He was becoming more and more difficult to ignore.

CHAPTER FIVE

THE sun was bright, reflecting off the pure white snow along the back porch. Even though it was March, deep drifts clung to the wooden latticework, making it look as if the house sat on a puff of cotton. Debra laughed as she remembered Andy's description. The boy was right.

Cuddling Betsy in a blanket, she looked off the porch toward her son, running in the snow and chasing birds looking for food. Having been cooped up in the house, he chomped at the bit when the weather dawned bright and relatively warm. She couldn't deny him some time to play outside.

She couldn't deny herself some time to watch him play. His giggles warmed her, as much as the swaddled baby she held in her arms.

"Look, Mommy, I made a heart with my footprints." Andy pointed to the random prints he'd made in the snow as he'd chased the birds, and sure enough, a heart appeared before her eyes.

She gave him a coy smile. "And who is the heart for?" She loved playing these games with him. She'd miss them when he got older.

"For you, Mommy!" He ran toward her and wrapped his arms around her legs in a three-year-old bear hug.

Debra leaned down to embrace her son when the monitor she'd stashed in her jacket pocket emitted a howl. John was calling.

She grabbed Andy and rushed into the house, ushering the boy in first. The screaming grew louder and more irritated as they entered the mudroom.

"Wipe your boots while I go see to John," she told Andy. Depositing Betsy in the playpen, she called, "I'm coming."

She rushed down the hall to John's room. "I'm sorry," she said as she opened the door. "Were you calling long? I was on the back porch."

"You left Betsy alone?" he asked, a darkness instantly shading his eyes.

"Of course not! She went outside with us."

"You took her outside? Why?"

"Because Andy wanted to play outside. Taking her with me seemed the reasonable thing to do." When was he going to trust her with his daughter? "Why were you calling?"

"Nothing. I didn't want anything. When will the guys be in?"

"Not until late, as usual. If you need something, you should tell me." She gave him a stern look.

"I need…I need to go to the bathroom," he muttered.

"Okay, if I support you, can you hop to the bathroom?" She hoped that would work.

"You're not going into the bathroom with me!"

"Believe me, I don't want to. All I'm offering is to get you there. You can…take care of business with the door closed. Then I'll help you back to bed."

He stared at her as he considered her words. "Okay."

She pulled back the covers.

"Hey!" John yelled, reaching for the blanket.

Debra gave him a superior look. "How are you going to get out of the bed with the covers still on?"

"I—I don't have my jeans on," he muttered, sounding lost. "Where are they?"

"I washed them today and I'll put them away until you start getting up. Then you can use them again, with the seams slit so your cast will fit."

"What are these?" he asked, touching the soft pajama bottoms.

"Don't you remember? I found them in your bottom drawer. I thought they'd be comfortable for you to sleep in and protect your modesty, too."

"Oh, yeah, I'd forgotten I had them."

"Can you swing your good leg to the floor?"

Since his right leg was the good one, he was able to put it on the floor without too much pain. She took his arm and put it around her shoulders. "Okay, now try to stand on your right leg. It will let your other leg come off the bed with less pain, I think."

He did as she asked, but from the wince on his face she knew pain raced through him. After a moment, he said, "Okay, let's go." They moved across the room, John hopping and leaning on Debra. When they got to the bathroom, she stayed with him until he reached the commode and could lean on the sink. Then she slipped back to the door, closing it after her.

Thank goodness, she thought. Feeling his big body against hers had affected her more than she'd thought it would. His scent, manly and woodsy, had filled her nostrils, too, making it impossible to think of anything but him. Even her legs had begun to be unsteady.

Several minutes later, he called her name. She slowly opened the door and entered to take his arm across her shoulders again to lead him back to the bed.

It was clear the effort had cost him. He lay back on his pillow, closing his eyes.

"John, you need to take off your shirt and replace it with a T-shirt. You'll be more comfortable, then. Can you do that?"

Slowly he opened his eyes and nodded. He began undoing his shirt and Debra turned to find the T-shirt she'd laid out earlier. When she turned back, John was lying against the pillow, his massive chest uncovered. Rippling muscles and six-pack abs stared her right in the face.

She licked her lips and straightened her shoulders, telling herself to avert her eyes. The command was hard to obey. She lowered her gaze to the T-shirt in her hand and held it out to him. Realizing he probably wouldn't be able to do it himself, she offered, "If you raise your arms, I'll help you put it on."

Now was when she wanted him to be stubborn and self-sufficient. Instead he acquiesced.

Keeping her head turned, she slid his shirt over his head and down his chest, proud that she hadn't made a fool of herself while doing so…until she realized John was essentially wrapped in her arms. Her heart thudded against her ribs and she pulled back from him as if he was a hot pot.

She wiped her hands down her jeans as if she could erase the feel of him and stepped back toward the door. "Would you like a snack? You can't have pain pills for another hour. How about a drink?" Damn, she was babbling like an embarrassed teenager. She took a deep breath to steady herself and looked up at him.

Luckily his eyes were closed so he hadn't seen her make a fool of herself. "Yeah," he said, "a snack would be good."

She fetched him a glass of milk and some cookies. "Shall I put some pillows behind you so you can drink without spilling it?" she asked as she reentered his room.

"Yeah, I guess so," he agreed, leaning forward. She propped him up, this time trying to avoid getting too close.

"Milk? Why did you bring me milk?"

"Because it goes well with cookies and it might help your bones."

"Hmm, okay, I guess I'll drink it."

"Do you need anything else?" Debra asked, seemingly reluctant to leave him alone. She kept her hands behind her back in case she was tempted to stroke that warm body again.

"I'd like to see Betsy," he said, his mouth full of cookies. As she turned to go get Betsy, he added, "These cookies are really good."

"Thank you," she said in surprise. Then she added, "I'll be right back."

She knew the difficulty she was going to face. As soon as Andy saw her, he asked what she was doing.

"I'm taking Betsy in to see her dad."

"I want to go see him, too."

"Andy, I'm not sure—" All the reasons he shouldn't get too attached to John marched into her brain, but her son's brown puppy-dog eyes slayed them all. "Okay. But he's having cookies for his snack, and you can't ask for any of them."

"Okay, Mommy. Will you give us cookies when we come back in here?"

"Yes, of course." She was beginning to wonder if her son was smarter than she was, having negotiated another snack.

She picked up Betsy, telling her she was going to go

see her daddy. Betsy cooperated by saying "Da-da" over and over again.

When they came into the bedroom, John looked up, surprise on his face to see Andy there. He didn't say anything that would hurt Andy's feelings, much to Debra's relief.

"Can I hold Betsy?" John asked.

"Of course, if you're not eating cookies. She'll try to eat them if you're not careful, and I don't want her to eat chocolate yet."

"Does Andy eat the chocolate chips?"

Before Debra could answer, her son emphatically responded. "Yes, I love them!"

John asked, "What else do you like?"

"I like cowboys."

"You do? We hadn't seen you much," he added.

"Mommy made me go to bed early. But she let me stay up last night, only you didn't come."

"I would've liked to, Andy, but a snake scared my horse and I fell off and broke my leg."

"Did the snake bite you?" Andy asked, his eyes big.

"No, I think he was as scared as my horse and he ran away."

"Da-da!" Betsy said, immediately drawing her father's attention. He had her sitting on his stomach.

"Hi, little girl. How are you doing?"

"She's really good at crawling. And she pulls herself up and bangs on the coffee table," Andy supplied.

"Is that so? Do you do that, Betsy?" John asked.

Betsy babbled at him again.

Debra, who was simply watching the interaction between the three, stepped in. "Yes, she does. She's a fast crawler, too."

"Good girl. I wish I could see you do all this amazing stuff," he said as he brought the baby down to his face so he could kiss her on the cheek. That movement also brought her closer to his cookies. She grabbed for them, spilling them on the bed.

Debra reached for her. "You'd better let me take her. Andy, can you help John pick up his cookies?"

Andy got a little too enthusiastic about picking up the cookies and lost his balance, landing in the middle of John's stomach. John yelped, which frightened Andy. He scrambled off the bed, tears welling in his eyes.

"I'm sorry, Mommy! I didn't mean to hurt him." Tears were running down the little boy's face.

"It's all right, Andy," Debra said, holding Betsy in one arm and reaching out with the other to comfort her son.

"Hey, Andy, I'm fine," John said, smiling at the little boy. "Don't cry. You were doing a good job of helping me. You just lost your balance. It's no big deal."

Debra couldn't believe how sensitive John was being to her son. She gave him a smile for the first time since they met in the church, one to match his smile. She'd been worried about how he'd interact with Andy, after that awful remark earlier. But he was being as sweet to Andy as he was to Betsy.

"You're all right?" Andy asked timidly.

"Sure I am," John replied. "Except for this dumb broken leg."

Debra stepped forward. "Now that we've established that everyone is all right, Andy, you need to come back into the living room. Betsy is going into her playpen, and I need to start planning dinner."

"Uh, Debra, can you ask Bill to come see me when he comes in?" John asked.

"Of course I can. But it will be a while, you know."

"Yeah, I know. I just wanted to ask you while you were in here."

"You're due for your medicine in half an hour. I'll be back to give it to you."

"No. I don't want it."

"Why?"

"Because it knocks me out." He looked away.

"It also helps you relax so your body can recover faster. Are you sure you don't want it?" She wanted what was best for him.

"I'm sure."

"All right. But I suggest you take the pill after you eat dinner. It'll help you sleep better." She didn't wait for an answer. She didn't want to hear any macho response that he could come up with.

When the men came in for dinner, she sent Bill back

to see John, asking him to encourage John to take his pills before bedtime that evening.

When Bill came back to the table, everyone else was eating.

"I made sure they left plenty for you, Uncle Bill," Debra teased him. "How did he seem to you?"

"Well, I think he's doing better. He doesn't like the pain pills 'cause they knock him out. But I told him he had to take them. He said to tell you he'd take them when you're ready."

"I'll take them to him now."

"Aren't you going to eat?"

"No, I ate earlier with the children."

She walked down the hall toward John's room, the pain pills in one hand and a glass of water in the other. Her heart was beating faster at the thought of spending time with John again. She'd taken him his dinner an hour ago. They'd had several pleasant exchanges, as if he didn't hate her anymore. In fact, he'd seemed downright friendly.

When she reached his bedroom, she noted that he'd clearly been out of bed. She would guess that her uncle had assisted him to the bathroom. She didn't have a problem with that, she guessed. After all, it was better if she didn't put her arm around him, or feel him pressing up against her. Wasn't it?

It had stopped any conflict between the two of them, at least.

"How are you doing, John?" she asked as she entered his bedroom.

"Fine. I enjoyed the meal you brought me."

More compliments. "Good. Here are your pills and some water."

"It's kind of early, isn't it?"

"By the time you get to sleep, it'll be nine o'clock. I think that's when you usually go to bed, isn't it?"

"Sometimes I stay up until ten."

"Do you want the men to move the television in here?"

He held up a hand. "No, that would be too much trouble."

"I'm sure they wouldn't mind."

"Well, if they don't mind…"

"I'll go ask." She was pleased that her suggestion made him happy.

When she reached the kitchen, the three cowhands had finished their meal and were sitting with Bill while he ate.

"John wondered if you'd move the television into his bedroom so he could watch it," she told them.

"Sure, we'd be glad to," Jess said, standing.

"Don't do that, boy." Bill's command stopped him. Everyone turned to stare at him.

"I've got a portable in the bunkhouse I don't use. If you'll go get it for me, Jess, I can connect it up."

"Sure, boss. I'll be right back."

Debra gave her uncle a peck on the cheek. "That's sweet of you, Uncle Bill."

"Never occurred to me the boy would want to watch television."

"I think it's because he's bored in bed all day."

"Maybe he should catch up on his paperwork. Of course, he hates doing it."

When Jess returned, Bill and the men took the TV into John's bedroom. By the time they emerged, Debra had the kitchen tidied. She picked up John's pills and water and went down the hall. "Ready for your medicine?"

"Not yet. I just turned on this program."

"John, I can't keep coming down here with the medicine you don't want to take." Because every time was a temptation to her, she didn't tell him.

"Then sit down for a few minutes. Maybe I'll get tired of the show and want to go to sleep."

Debra gave him an exaggerated sigh and sat down in the chair closest to the bed. "What kind of show is this?"

"I don't know exactly. I think it may be a mystery. Have you seen it?"

"No. I used to go to bed early because I had to get up at four-thirty."

"You mean you weren't lying when you said you got up that early?"

Debra returned his surprised stare. "No. Why would I lie about that?"

"Because I was giving you a hard time. I figured you made it up to make me feel bad."

"But it didn't make you feel bad, did it?"

"No, because I figured you were lying."

They both laughed and Debra sat back to watch the TV. On screen, a curvaceous blonde crept into a shadowy room. Moving to a bedside, she started unbelting her coat as she spoke to the man on the bed. When he didn't respond, she reached over to touch him and then screamed bloody murder.

"Are you sure this isn't a comedy?" she asked.

He rolled his eyes at her. "Is that what you'd think if you found someone dead?"

"I'm going up to bed now, John. I'll leave your pills and water on the table here beside you."

"Did I upset you?" John asked, watching her.

"No. I'm just tired, so I think I'll go on to bed. Remember to take your pills." She turned out his light. "Good night."

"Good night," he replied. Then, "Uh, Debra?" She turned back to him. "I—I wanted to say…thanks for helping me today."

She nodded in acceptance, then turned and practically ran from the room as if the hounds of hell were nipping at her heels. If she didn't, even in the dark, John would see the attraction she was working so hard to hide.

Somehow, getting out of bed the next morning was easier for Debra. She still knew she had to prepare for the future, but John wasn't an enemy anymore. That made her life easier. And harder. She wouldn't be fighting with him anymore, she didn't think, but she'd be fighting with herself.

She opened his door without turning on a light, just to check on him. He wasn't tossing and turning, but she leaned closer and noted a frown on his face. She fought the urge to lean over and kiss it away. After a moment, she went to the kitchen to get his medicine.

Entering his bedroom again, she left the door open so the hall light shone into the room. Then she sat down on the bed beside him. "John? Time to take your pills."

"What?" he muttered.

"Open up so I can give you your pills."

He automatically opened his mouth, and she popped the pills in.

"Good job. Now raise up and take a drink of water."

He did that, too, but it seemed to wake him up. "What are you doing?"

"I just gave you your medicine so you could continue sleeping without pain."

"What time is it?"

"It's a little after five. There's no need for you to get up early." Suddenly she realized her arm was still around his shoulders, supporting him for his drink of water. She gently slid her arm out from under him and his head fell back to the pillow.

"I need to talk to Bill before he goes out."

"Why?"

"I need to know how things are going."

Soothingly she said, "I'll find out for you. You just go back to sleep." She stroked his forehead, trying to wipe away that frown. When he seemed to doze off again, she breathed a sigh of relief. Relief that she could stop touching him. She was getting too involved with John, and she knew he was going to get rid of her when he hired a housekeeper.

"Wait!" John called as she turned to go to the kitchen.

Afraid something was wrong, she came back to his bedside. "What is it, John? Is it the pain? Are you still hurting?" She waited anxiously for him to explain what he needed.

"No—no, I need—" Then it appeared he fell asleep.

"John, what do you need?

"I need…"

Debra knelt closer. "John, if you'll tell me what you need, I'll get it for you."

His hand snaked around her neck. She tried to move back, but he held her firmly.

"John, what—"

Then he told her. It was a mumble, but she clearly understood him.

And he gave her no choice. He pulled her mouth to his just after he said, "I need a kiss."

CHAPTER SIX

DEBRA had breakfast ready on time, without making any mistakes. She felt rather bewildered by what had happened with John. But she decided to put that surprising event away, to wash it from her memory, because she was sure John wouldn't remember. But it wouldn't be easy.

When the men came in for breakfast, she asked Bill to write out something telling John how things were going. "I think he's feeling left out," she explained.

"Do I have to write it? Can't I just go talk to him?"

"Well, he took some pills when I got up. He was in pain."

"You didn't have trouble convincing him?" Bill asked.

Debra felt her cheeks heating up and she bent over the stove, hoping the men would think the heat was coming from the stove. "No, he didn't really wake up. So it was easy."

"So he won't be waking up anytime soon?"

"No, Bill, I think he'll sleep until about ten o'clock."

Jess came to Debra's rescue. "Boss, I can write down what you want to say. Debra, you got some paper and a pen?"

"Yes, I'll go get it." She was glad to get out of the kitchen. She was afraid someone would realize what had happened with John.

After the men left for work, with a note written by Jess for John to let him know how things were proceeding, Debra took an unusual break. She poured herself a cup of coffee and actually ate a couple of pancakes. She'd been skipping meals and snacking rather than actually eating. But this morning, she needed something in her stomach.

Her husband had left her before the baby was born. Since then, Debra had remained celibate. She'd had her son to raise and a job that exhausted her. She didn't even consider going out. So she hadn't been kissed by a man in over three years. And it would probably be as long again, she chided herself. Today had been an accident. John probably thought he was kissing his dead wife.

From all accounts, he'd truly loved her. The woman was an idiot to choose to run away, leaving a good man and a beautiful baby. After all, she didn't have to do the cooking or the cleaning. She only had to please her husband, who was blindly in love with her, and take care of Betsy.

Debra closed her eyes, thinking about what it would mean to be loved by a strong man, a man she could count on, could admire. A man who wanted to share his life with her. A vision of her in John's arms filled her with joy and excitement, causing a shiver to run through her body.

Then she opened her eyes and she put away that vision. It was only imaginary.

"Oh, well," she muttered and took another sip of coffee. She heard Betsy waking up, and she hurried upstairs to the baby. "Good morning, Betsy," she cooed. "How are you this morning?"

"Ma-ma!" Betsy greeted her.

"Yes, sweetheart, it's Mama." She lifted the baby up so she could kiss her cheek. Then she laid her down to change her diaper. Once that was done, she took the baby in her arms and tiptoed into Andy's room to see if her son was waking up.

He stirred as she watched. "Andy? Are you ready to get up? I've got breakfast almost ready."

"Okay," Andy agreed. Then he closed his eyes again.

"Sweetie, that means it's time to get up. Go wash your face and I'll put out some clothes for you to wear." As she did so, she noted that Andy was outgrowing what he had. She was going to have to sell a quilt just to keep him in clothes.

Once she had both kids in the kitchen, she made pancakes for Andy and mixed cereal for Betsy. Betsy looked at her breakfast and then at Andy's and reached for his.

"No, Betsy, you need to eat your cereal." After she put

a spoonful of cereal in Betsy's mouth, she added, "I'll give you a bite of pancake after you eat your breakfast.

Suddenly she heard John's voice. "Uh, Andy, can you please go tell John I'll bring his breakfast as soon as I finish feeding Betsy?"

"Sure, Mommy." Andy hopped down from his chair and ran out of the room.

Debra was afraid he needed her support to get to the bathroom, and that would involve touching. She was hoping to avoid that.

She strained her ears, trying to hear what John said to Andy, but other than a low rumble, she could hear nothing. She had to wait till Andy came back down the hall. When he slid into his seat, she asked, "What did John say?"

"He said okay."

"That's all he said? Did he need help getting to the bathroom?"

"He didn't say anything," Andy said, looking at his mother curiously.

Then they all heard a big crash.

Debra was on the move almost at once. "Andy, stay here and keep an eye on Betsy. Don't let her climb out of the high chair!" She raced down the hall to John's room.

As she expected, she found him on the floor halfway to the bathroom. "John! Did you hurt yourself?"

He managed to roll over and gave her an ugly look. "It sure didn't help anything!"

Debra straightened. "I beg your pardon, but I was

feeding Betsy her breakfast. If you couldn't wait, you should've told Andy."

"I know, I know," John said in disgust. "But I thought I could make it on my own."

"Let me get you up. Then I'll help you to the bathroom, like we did yesterday."

"Thanks."

He didn't sound grateful, but Debra dismissed that thought. She suggested he get on his good knee and she'd help him stand. They managed to get him upright and Debra slipped his arm around her shoulder and put her arm around his waist. She felt his warmth up and down her body.

"You okay?" he asked as they reached the bathroom door. "You seem out of breath."

"I—I'm fine. I was just afraid you'd hurt yourself."

"I'm okay."

"Good. I'll wait for you here."

She breathed a deep sigh when the door was closed between them. If he didn't get his walking cast on soon, she might attack him right here in his bed. Was she that starved for love? She smiled at herself in derision. It wasn't love. At least she didn't think so. It was plain old lust.

When he opened the door, she helped him back to bed. "I'm going to go finish feeding Betsy. Then I'll bring you a breakfast tray. Do you want more medicine? It might be a good idea in case your fall makes you sore."

"No, I don't want any more medicine. Did you give

me pills this morning? Otherwise, I don't think I'd sleep this late."

"Yes, I did, because you were in pain. I have to go now."

She hurried out of the room before he could say anything else. The last thing she wanted to discuss was their early morning encounter.

When she reached the kitchen, she found Andy standing beside Betsy's high chair, feeding her. "Oh, Andy, thank you, sweetheart."

"Look, Mommy, I can do it just like you do. But she's hungry and she tries to take the spoon away from me."

"I know she does. Here, I'll finish feeding her. Go eat." Andy went back to his pancakes. "Is John okay?"

"Um, yes, I think so. He fell down, but he said he didn't hurt his leg again. I'll be glad when he gets his cast."

"A cast? Will he let me sign it?"

"How do you know about signing a cast?"

"I saw it on TV."

"Oh. Well, I don't know. And I don't know when he'll get his cast. But it will make my life easier." And it would stop her from having to touch him. He was a big, strong man. The kind that could hold you in his arms and make you feel safe. She'd never had that feeling, but it was something she longed for.

Later, when she made John's breakfast, she asked her son, "Andy, would you like to go say hello to John?"

"Yeah, Mommy. I'll ask him if I can sign his cast!"

"Okay," Debra agreed. She would've agreed to anything as long as she didn't have to face John alone. She didn't want any questions about this morning's activity.

"I'll take Betsy and you can come with us. I think John will like that."

She wiped Betsy's hands and face and picked her up from the high chair. "Do you want to go see Daddy?"

The baby immediately began to babble "Da-da."

"Good girl," Debra whispered. She went down the hall, Andy in front of her. When they got to John's room, he had the television on.

"Hi, John!" Andy said, greeting him with a big smile.

"Hi, Andy. How are you this morning?"

"Good. Can I sign your cast when you get one?"

Debra shook her head. Her son always went right to the question he had on his mind. No manipulation on his part.

"Sure. That would be great. Uh, can you write your name?"

"Part of it. Mommy is teaching me," Andy said with a glance to her over his shoulder.

John followed his gaze and realized she was there, along with his daughter. "Betsy! You came to see me, too? I'm a lucky guy, aren't I?"

"Yes, you are," Debra said. "Can you handle holding Betsy for a moment, and I'll go get your breakfast tray?"

"Good, I'm starving," he said, holding out his arms for his child.

Debra made sure he had a good hold on the wriggly

baby before she left the room. She didn't want any more accidents.

She brought his tray, with the note folded carefully beside the silverware, so he'd see it at once.

After she set his tray on the lamp table, she reached out for Betsy. The baby greeted her with a loud "Ma-ma!"

Debra quickly looked at John. He was frowning.

"I didn't teach her that. She heard it from Andy."

John nodded. "I figured," he said.

Uncomfortable, Debra pointed at the tray. "There's a note from Bill. I told him you wanted to know what was going on."

"Are you sure it's from Bill?"

"Why would you ask that?"

"Because Bill can't write much," John said as he unfolded the note.

"I didn't know that."

"Yeah, I wrote most of his notes to you and your mom. I thought maybe you knew."

"No. I never saw the letters."

"But you did get the money, didn't you?" John asked.

"No," Debra said. "Eat your breakfast before it gets cold."

He took a bite, but it didn't stop the questions. "Why didn't you get the money? I know Bill sent it every month."

"He sent it to my mother. She never told me."

"Your own mother did that to you?"

"Not all women are cut out to be mothers, John. She was very self-absorbed. She also took all of my paycheck. I got to keep my share of the tip money since I never told her about that. But it didn't amount to much."

"You worked hard all that time and she took your entire paycheck? What for?"

"Andy and I shared her small apartment and she looked after him while I worked."

"I see."

"Eat your breakfast, John."

Before he did as she ordered, he asked one more question. "You aren't going to leave, are you?"

She stared at him. That was the first time he'd ever requested her presence. "I—I guess we can stay a few minutes, if that's what you want."

"Good. Did you read the note?"

"I didn't need to. Bill dictated it to Jess."

"Good for Jess. I guess he knows Bill can't read and write very well. But he sure knows ranching."

"I see."

"Did you go to college?"

"No. I got pregnant with Andy during my senior year in high school. By the time I graduated from high school, I'd been married and widowed."

"What happened to your husband?"

"He found marriage to be too confining and a job too hard to hold, so he quit me and the job and took up drug-dealing."

"Not exactly a safe job. Didn't he care about his child?"

Debra looked at her son, playing with Betsy. "No, he was too young."

"How old were you?"

"I was eighteen."

"I don't suppose you got any insurance when he died."

"No one insures drug dealers."

"I'm sorry, Debra. I had no idea—I mean, I knew Bill was sending you what he could. I imagined you were leading a nice life. I had no idea life was so bad for you. It's my fault Bill stopped sending the money. He told me I could keep most of his salary until we got back on our feet."

Debra shrugged her shoulders. "It doesn't matter. We survived. And nothing could make me regret my son."

"Yeah. I guess we have a lot in common."

"I guess so. Do you need more breakfast?" she asked.

Anything to distract him from her life. She didn't like talking about her past. She'd made some bad choices, but she wouldn't redo them if it meant not having Andy. She loved her son so much.

"It's funny, isn't it?" John said.

"What?"

"My wife had an easy life, but it wasn't enough. She spent a lot of money, trying to find happiness, but she felt she had to leave. I guess she didn't really love me."

He sounded sad. Debra couldn't resist patting his shoulder. "I think she probably loved you as much as she could, but she sounds a lot like my mother. She was only focused on herself, and even Betsy wasn't enough to hold her."

He took a sip of his coffee before he said anything else. Then he smiled at her. "Thanks, Debra, for trying to make me feel better. I've been a little bitter over my lot in life. I resisted doing what Bill suggested, but it looks like he was right. You've been a big help."

Yes, she'd done well as a fill-in. But in the fall, he'd hire a housekeeper. Debra was beginning to realize how painful it would be to leave.

"I've got to clean up the kitchen. Andy, are you ready?"

"Okay, Mommy. Bye, John," her son said readily. She reached for Betsy, but John held on to his daughter.

"What are you going to do with Betsy while you clean the kitchen?"

"I'll put her in her playpen with Andy watching *Sesame Street*. She even likes the show, and it keeps them both entertained."

"I've got a television in here. They could stay here with me."

"Are you sure you want to watch a children's show?"

"Yeah, I'll get to see what Betsy is watching. And if I have trouble understanding it, Andy can explain it to me. Right, Andy?"

"Sure. Can we, Mommy?"

"I—I suppose so. I'll go get Betsy's playpen."

Once she had them set up, she ordered Andy not to

get on the bed before the familial scene in front of her proved too enticing to resist.

John lay back against the pillows. In spite of his broken leg, he felt good. He might even say happy. The kids were in here with him; he didn't have to go anywhere. He could just relax, with a full stomach.

"Hey, John, look, it's Cookie Monster!"

"Does he scare you?" John asked curiously, looking at the blue furry puppet.

"No. He doesn't scare anybody. He just loves cookies, like me!" The little boy chuckled.

"If the cookies are some your mommy made, I think I'm a cookie monster, too."

Andy giggled.

"Why don't you come sit on the bed, Andy? It's got to be more comfortable than down there on the floor. You're going to get a crick in your neck, if you don't."

"But Mommy said—"

"I'll tell Mommy I invited you. She won't mind."

Andy agreed and climbed up on the bed. John put him on his right side, so the boy couldn't accidentally bump into his bad leg. Then he shared his pillows with him, and they settled down to watch Andy's favorite show.

But John wasn't really watching the show. He was thinking about Andy's mother. What a hard life she'd had. And how sad it was that her mother kept all the money Bill had been sending her.

She'd probably ended up pregnant because she was looking for the affection she'd obviously not found at home. Then he thought about his own little girl. If Elizabeth had lived, she would've been like Debra's mother. But already he could tell Debra was loving to Betsy.

"Da-da!" Betsy squealed, trying to reach him over the top of the playpen. Was she jealous that Andy was on the bed and she wasn't? His child was developing fast.

"Debra?" he called.

Andy immediately sat up. "Why did you call Mommy?"

"I think Betsy wants to get up here with us," John said.

"Maybe I should get down," Andy said and started scooting toward the edge of the bed.

"No, Andy, it's all right, I promise." He could hear Debra coming down the hall.

"Yes, John?" she asked as she came through the door. Then she saw Andy on the bed. "Andy, I told you to stay on the floor."

"I'm sorry, Mommy—" Andy began.

"Debra, it's my fault, not Andy's. I asked him to come up here with me. He hasn't bothered me at all."

"Then why did you call me?"

"I wondered if it would be all right if Betsy joined us? She seems jealous that she's in her playpen and Andy is up here with me."

"I think the easier solution would be for Andy to get back on the floor."

John grinned. "I don't like that idea. It's kind of nice to have someone in bed with me. I was feeling too isolated before."

Debra blinked at that statement and had to bite her tongue not to volunteer to join him there, minus the kids.

Betsy added to the mix by chanting, "Da-da."

Debra sighed. "All right, for a few minutes. It will be time for her bath soon, anyway. Are you sure you can handle both of them?"

"Yeah, and Andy will help me."

"All right, but don't turn loose of her. She might fall off the bed."

"I promise," he said, adding a big smile.

She gave him a strange look before she lifted Betsy from the playpen and put her on the bed between Andy and John. Then she looked at her son. "Don't let Betsy get past you, okay?"

"Okay, Mommy."

She looked at John. "If he forgets because he's watching television, make him help you."

"It's not a problem, Debra. We'll be fine." John smiled at her again. He found it interesting that his smiles didn't seem to make her relax. If anything, she seemed to tense up. Why? He knew they'd gotten off to a bad start, but things were improving, weren't they? Didn't she think so?

He was even spending time with Andy. And enjoying it. What else did she want from him?

Maybe she was just too overworked. How could he lessen her burden? He'd have to think about that, because he wanted her to be happy.

What was the matter with him? He'd tried to make his wife happy and had failed miserably. What made him think he could do anything to impress Debra?

CHAPTER SEVEN

DEBRA was bathing Betsy when the phone rang. She didn't bother trying to answer. John had a phone by his bed.

Betsy squealed and splashed Debra again. "You naughty girl," Debra said with a smile, wiping her face with a towel she'd laid out for that purpose. She'd discovered early on that the little girl loved her baths.

"Debra?" John called.

She was beginning to wish John didn't know her name. But he'd still call someone. With a sigh, she called back, "I'm bathing Betsy!"

She continued her task, shampooing Betsy's hair. As she did so, she heard steps on the stairs. She was pretty sure it was Andy. Who else could it be? He must be the message runner this morning. She wrapped Betsy in a towel and gently dried her off as Andy burst into the room.

"Mommy, that was the doctor who called. He wants John to come get his cast on this morning!"

"I'm not sure we can do that, Andy. I'll come talk to John as soon as I get Betsy dressed."

"Okay, I'll go tell him." Andy dashed out the door as if he were carrying a special message to the president. It worried Debra that he was so involved in John's situation.

Like her.

She diapered Betsy and dressed her in fresh clothes. Then she brushed her hair and put in a barrette. She might be ready for a haircut, soon, but Debra wasn't sure her daddy would agree.

"Come on, Betsy. Let's go visit with your daddy again."

"Da-da," Betsy repeated all the way down the stairs. When they reached the bedroom, Andy was on the bed with John, chatting away.

John looked up as they came in. "Who is Eileen?"

Debra came to an abrupt halt. "Why?"

"Andy mentioned her. I just wondered."

"She's my mother. Do you want to hold Betsy a minute? She just had her bath."

"Sure. Come here, Betsy," John said, opening his arms to his child. That was one thing Debra had noted about John. He was always willing to hold his child.

"Andy said the doctor wants you to come in this morning to get your cast on?"

"This morning or this afternoon. He thinks the swelling should have gone down enough and it's safer to get the cast on as soon as possible. That way I can get to the bathroom on my own," he added with a smile.

"Shall I call Uncle Bill on the walkie-talkie and get him to come in?"

John raised an eyebrow. "Why? Can't you drive me in?"

Debra stared at him. "We'd have two others accompanying us," she said, looking at the two children. "Do you think that's wise?"

"If you can handle them while I'm getting my cast on, I think we can manage. My truck has a second row for their car seats. Plus, if you need to do any shopping afterward, I'll be able to help with them."

Debra nodded. "Then I guess we can."

"Can you get my ripped up jeans and a shirt for me?"

"Yes, of course. I'll put them in the bathroom." She opened his closet and grabbed the jeans, then she selected at blue knit shirt that would match his eyes.

"All right," she said after putting Betsy in the playpen. "Let's get you to the bathroom."

"Are we in a rush?" he asked as he reached for her support in getting off the bed.

"Yes. The kids will need to have lunch and then take their naps as soon as we get home."

"Oh, I see. I'll hurry."

"Mommy, do I get to go?" Andy asked, his eyes glowing.

"Yes, honey, but you have to be very good. I won't be able to carry you because I'll need to carry Betsy."

"I'm a big boy, Mommy. I can walk."

"Thank you, sweetie. I appreciate that."

John opened the bathroom door, frowning. "Why did you pick this shirt, Deb?"

"I liked the color. Why? Don't you like it?" She wondered about the funny look on his face. "I'll get another one if—"

"My first wife bought it for me, that's all," he explained. "But don't worry, it's fine. Come on. We need to go."

It only took a couple of minutes before he hopped out of the bathroom. "I'm ready."

"All right. Wait here till I get the kids settled."

Moving at a good pace, she put both car seats into John's truck in the garage, then came back for the kids. As she was strapping a squirming Betsy into the seat, she suddenly remembered a necessity. "Andy, can you run upstairs and get the diaper bag? It's been so long since you were a baby, I forgot I needed it."

Then she ran into the kitchen for a spare bottle. When she came back out to the truck, Betsy immediately grabbed for it. "Not now, Betsy," she said gently, moving it out of sight. "This is for later."

Andy ran into the garage, the bag almost as big as he was. "Here it is, Mommy."

"Thank you, sweetie. Now get in your seat." Andy knew the drill and snapped the belt of his car seat all by himself.

Next, Debra headed back to the bedroom for John. This was the last time she'd have to touch him, she realized. After this, he'd have the walking cast on and be back to the self-sufficient man he was. She almost savored the experience as he reached out to rest his arm on her shoulder as he stood on one leg.

"Ready?" she asked as she slid her arm around his waist. She held him tight until she got him settled into the truck. "When I close the door, you can lean against it and extend your leg on the seat."

He did as she advised and the nearness of his leg to her distracted her from her driving. That, and the fact that his eyes never left her. She could feel them running up and down her side. At the same time she wanted to tell him to stop, but relished the attention. She settled on trying harder to focus on the road, deciding in the end that his glances were worse than Andy's usual endless litany of questions from the back seat.

Fifteen minutes later, she pulled to a stop in front of a small doctor's office on the outskirts of Westlake. Betsy was asleep so she'd take John in, first, then come back out for the children. She came around to the passenger side to help him but he'd already swung his legs around.

"I'll get myself out," he insisted. "Then you can help me in." But his good leg was more wobbly than he thought, and Debra reached out just in time to duck under his arm and hold him up. Together they made it to the front door.

The nurse behind the desk came immediately to help.

"We're so glad you made it in today, John. The doctor will be out of town tomorrow. Let's just go right on in to the examining room, if you don't mind, Miss…"

Debra was about to supply her name when John spoke up. "Ellen, this is my wife, Debra."

"Then it's true. There's a rumor going around that you got married again, but I'd heard you swear that would never happen, so I wasn't sure." Ellen stopped as they reached the examining table. "Can you use your good leg and sit down up there, John?" She turned to Debra. "My, you're a good assistant. John is lucky to have you."

"Thank you," Debra said with a faint smile. "I need to go get the kids out of the truck now, if that's all right."

"Kids? There's more than Betsy? I guess you have children, too?"

"A three-year-old son."

"That's wonderful. Now you have both a boy and a girl."

"Yes. If you'll excuse me—"

"Of course."

Debra went to get the children, Betsy fussing from having been woken from her nap. As soon as she got in the waiting room and took her bottle, she settled down immediately. Like a little soldier, Andy sat quietly in the adjacent chair. He watched Ellen's every move when the nurse came out from the back to answer the ringing phone.

"Isn't she supposed to be taking care of John?" he asked.

"I'm sure the doctor is with him, now," Debra whispered.

The nurse hung up the phone and looked at them. "My, Betsy has certainly grown. Is she doing all right?" She rose and came over from her desk.

Debra took the bottle out of Betsy's mouth and helped her sit up. The baby frowned and reached for the bottle. "Ba-ba-ba-ba."

"Oh, listen to her talk! My, she's growing fast, isn't she?"

"Yes, I guess so."

"And this must be your son."

"His name is Andy."

"Well, hello, Andy. I'm Ellen. Welcome to Westlake. Do you like it here?"

Debra held her breath as her son decided how to answer that question.

"I think so," he said with a grin.

"We haven't been here but about a week," Debra explained.

"Of course, I should've known that. You know, it's strange but I didn't hear about John's engagement, then he turns up married." Not skipping a beat, she turned back to Andy. "Don't worry, Andy, you'll like it just fine after you've been here a while."

Debra wasn't sure they'd be here long enough for

Andy to find out if he really liked it. But she was beginning to realize they would be here long enough for Andy's heart to be broken when he had to leave John. Just like hers.

Discussing Betsy's care with Ellen helped pass the time as they waited for John. After a half hour, the doctor emerged from the back. He was tall, with a well-groomed dark beard and a lab coat over cords and a plaid shirt. "I wanted to meet the new Mrs. Richey. How do you do, ma'am? I'm Dr. Harms. Welcome to Westlake."

"Thank you, Doctor. How's our patient?"

"He'll be out shortly. Just thought I'd come out and meet the woman John's been talking about."

So, Debra thought, John was talking about her? She'd give a fortune to find out what he'd said.

The middle-aged doctor leaned down and smiled at Betsy. "She looks good. Whatever you're doing is fine, Debra. I hope you don't mind me calling you that."

"Of course not, Doctor."

"Well, feel free to call me Tom. Everyone does. We're a small community, here. I answer questions over the phone all the time and they're not always about medical things, either."

Debra laughed with the doctor. "I'll remember that, Tom."

"Since you're here, Betsy needs a couple of shots. Can we do that now?"

"I guess so, if it's all right with John."

"He agreed. Would you bring Betsy back to my office?"

"Of course. Andy—"

"He can come along and I'll let him visit with John, who is bored to tears. Is that okay, Andy?"

"Yes. I like to visit with John," Andy said.

The shots only took a couple of minutes, but Betsy cried a lot. Debra thanked the doctor even as she soothed Betsy.

"We're lucky that Betsy has remained healthy," Tom said. "I think it's because she never sees other babies."

"I think you're right, Tom. But now she'll be more protected. When shall I bring her in again?"

"When she's a year old." He opened his office door. "Now, I'd better go check on your husband. He should be ready to go in a few minutes. And I'll congratulate him. His upgrade in the wife department is quite superior."

"Thank you," Debra said, her cheeks flushing even as she willed them not to. Tom noticed, unfortunately, because he laughed as he walked across the hall.

Oh, my. She hadn't thought about meeting the residents of Westlake. They all liked John, it seemed, and welcomed her warmly. If only they knew what kind of marriage she and John had. It was going to be awkward when John dumped her in the fall. But that would be his problem, not hers, she reminded herself.

As if thoughts of the man conjured up the real thing, John appeared through the open doorway of the office across the hall. He walked out on a huge white walking cast from his toes to his thigh.

Debra couldn't measure her relief. No more pressing up against him to help him walk. He could manage on his own, now.

He stopped in front of her. "What do you think? Pretty spiffy, isn't it?"

"Very spiffy. I hope you thanked Tom properly. He's certainly made my life easier."

John's eyebrows soared. "You make it sound like I was difficult to deal with!"

Debra grinned. "You outweigh me by a hundred pounds and I had to support you for you to get out of bed. You think that was easy?"

John put his hands on her face and bent down and kissed her, shocking her into silence.

"Probably not, but you never complained. Ready to go?"

She was ready, all right. Ready to jump him. He looked so incredibly handsome, his smile making his eyes crinkle just the way she loved.

"Uh, yes. I'm ready."

"Me, too," Andy said, coming out from behind John. "And I'm starving!"

"So am I, Andy. Let's go to the café for lunch," John suggested.

Debra stared at John. Who was this man grinning at her? Inviting her to lunch in a public place? He seemed light-years away from the surly, brooding boor she'd married. "I'm not sure that's a good idea, John," she whispered.

"Why not?"

"Let's discuss it in the truck." She leaned around John. "Thank you again, Tom."

"Call anytime you need me."

"Thank you, I will."

On the way out she reached out a hand for Andy but John stopped her.

"Andy's going to take my hand. He'll help keep me balanced," John said, smiling at her son.

Once they were in the truck, John pressed her for an answer. "So, tell me why we can't go to the café."

She looked at him. "I'm not sure meeting more residents of Westlake right now is a good idea."

"There won't be many there in the middle of the day. Now, on Saturday night, I could understand your reluctance, but we'll probably be the only ones there for lunch."

"Then why do they stay open?"

"They do a big breakfast and dinner business." As if he hadn't heard her refusal, he said to Andy, "They have great hamburgers and fries. Does that sound good?"

Andy's eyes grew big. "Like McDonald's?"

"Just as good, I swear!"

"Oh, please, Mommy!"

Debra surrendered. "Fine, but you have to pay," she told John. "I don't have any money."

"Of course I'll pay. I'm the dad, right, Andy?"

"Yeah!"

She wished Betsy were old enough to vote. But maybe not. The little girl was already showing a tendency toward her father and his wishes. Just like Andy.

Pulling the truck across the street, she parked it and got out, coming around to get Betsy.

"I've got her. Get Andy out over there," John called.

Debra hurried Andy out of the truck. She still wasn't sure John had his balance in control. It would be terrible if he fell holding Betsy.

When she reached the other side of the truck, John was laughing at her. "You didn't think I could do it, did you? Come on, Debra, confess."

"You're right. I didn't think—that is, I thought you might have some trouble. I didn't want Betsy to get hurt."

"Me, neither," John said. He shifted Betsy to his other hand and slipped his arm around Debra's shoulders. "Andy, are you there?"

"Yes, John," the boy said.

They entered the restaurant like that, looking like a happy family of four.

"Do we wait to be seated?" Debra asked in a whisper.

John laughed. "If we did, we'd be here all day. Pick a table."

Debra chose one by the window set for four. She found a high chair and John put Betsy in it.

Then, when Debra thought he would sit down, he

walked to the counter and rang a cowbell a couple of times. "Hello! You've got some business out here."

A robust man with a full head of thick white curls ambled out of a side door. "John? What are you doing in town in the middle of the day?"

"Looking for lunch, Baldy. We've been to the doctor's office to get my cast on. Now I've brought my family over here for lunch."

"Your family? All those belong to you?" Before John could answer, the man stuck his head back in the door. "Hey, Lucy, Aggie, come out here and meet John's family."

Now Debra knew for sure they'd made a mistake in coming here.

CHAPTER EIGHT

JOHN introduced his new family to his old friends. It amazed him how pleased he was to do so. Of course, the threesome had seen Betsy before, but they hadn't expected to meet Debra and Andy so soon.

Debra was charming, blushing whenever they complimented her. He thought back to the one time he'd brought Elizabeth to the café. She'd sneered at his friends and embarrassed him. He'd never made that mistake again.

With Debra, everything seemed so much easier. She did all the work he asked of her and more. When he'd needed help, she hadn't hesitated to come to his aid, even when he was grumpy. And she treated his daughter as if she really was her child.

Elizabeth had been beautiful on the outside, but that beauty had dimmed as he'd learned her true nature. Debra hadn't impressed him when he'd seen her at their bare-bones wedding. But she was growing more beautiful every day, because her beauty came from the inside.

After chatting with the threesome, they placed their orders.

"We can make some creamed peas, too, if you want," Aggie suggested. "They're our specialty."

"That would be lovely, if you don't mind," Debra told the woman. Aggie was slim, fit and nearing seventy, but she appeared to have the energy of a teenager.

"I'll take some, too, Aggie," John said. "And don't forget those French fries for me and Andy."

"Not a chance," Baldy said, grinning. "They're the best part."

Lucy, instead of following the other two to the kitchen, stayed put, her arm on the back of John's chair. "So, how did the two of you meet?"

Debra turned a bright red.

Before she could answer, John spoke up. "We met through the mail. We've been exchanging letters for a while."

"Letters? My goodness, you sure took a chance, John. But I think you got lucky," she added, winking at Debra.

"Come on, Lucy, you could say she got lucky to end up with an upstanding man like me," John mock-protested.

"Yeah, I could." Lucy's laughter hung in the air as she left the table to go to the kitchen.

"We wrote letters?" Debra asked, her cheeks still red. She looked cautiously at her son, but he was playing with Betsy.

John shrugged. "I had to think fast. That was the best I could come up with on short notice. Besides, it's almost the truth. I wrote Bill's letters to your mother."

"Which I never saw."

"Honey, if I'd told the truth, it would've really embarrassed you."

"I think it might've embarrassed you, too."

"Maybe so," he agreed with a grin.

But he didn't feel embarrassed now. In fact, pride filled his chest as he surveyed his family. Yeah, he was coming to realize he was a lucky man.

Once he would've said he had the worst luck in the world. The only good thing in his life had been Betsy. Come to think of it, Betsy had brought Debra and Andy into his life.

"What are you thinking about?" Debra asked, surprising him.

"About how lucky I am."

She looked at him, but she said nothing. She didn't talk a lot. That was another difference between her and Elizabeth. Elizabeth had talked a lot, constantly. But it was always about her and her desires. She'd never asked about anyone else and was bored if the conversation wasn't centered on her. He'd been so enamored of her that he'd assumed she'd change. He was wrong.

She wasn't even that good in bed. He'd been sure making love with Elizabeth would've been the best. But she'd turned out to be a selfish lover and not all that interested in it much. She'd teased him until they were married. Then she'd felt she'd done her duty on their wedding night and that should have been enough.

As Debra sipped her drink, John gazed at her. He hadn't thought he'd be interested in sleeping with his second wife. That was another mistake he'd made. And one he was thinking a lot about the past several days.

What did she think about it?

She was eyeing him suspiciously right now. Not a good sign. He needed to let her know how much he appreciated her. His earlier idea about taking some of the work off her slender shoulders was a good one.

"I think we should go by the store after this," he said.

Her eyes widened. "Why?"

"I need to look at some things. Do you need anything?" He knew her wardrobe wasn't extensive. She'd only been there a little over a week, and she'd repeated most everything she'd worn.

"No, nothing."

"What about the kids?"

"Betsy needs some new outfits. She's growing and the season is changing."

"Good. You can shop for Betsy. What about Andy?"

"No, he's fine."

"He's not growing?"

"I'll take care of him later."

"Andy, could you come here?" John asked. The little boy slid out of his chair and stood next to John.

"What is it, John?"

"I wanted to show your mom something."

"What?" Andy asked.

"I wanted to show your mom what a good job you're doing in the growing department."

"I'm getting bigger. Mommy says I'm outgrowing my jeans too fast, didn't you, Mommy?"

"You're doing just fine, sweetie." Debra smiled at her son. When Andy went back to playing with Betsy again, Debra glared at John and whispered, "I don't have the money right now. But I will, and I'll buy Andy more jeans then."

Okay, he'd proved his point. Debra didn't want him to pay for her or Andy. "How are you going to earn that money?"

"It doesn't matter as long as I do everything you ask of me." That warm, open expression she wore when she dealt with the kids was gone.

"Debra, I can pay for some clothes for all three of you. There's no reason to wait."

She ignored him.

Just then, Baldy, Aggie and Lucy came out of the kitchen with their orders.

"Oh, my, Andy, that hamburger is almost as big as you!" Debra exclaimed. "The French fries alone would be enough to fill you up. I don't know how you'll eat all that."

Andy's eyes were big. "Me, neither," he muttered.

"Don't worry, Andy," John said. "I'll help you out in that department. Just in case you need it."

"Thank you, John."

John wanted to hug the little boy, but he was afraid Debra would make a big deal about it. But Andy had his mother's sweetness. And her charm.

With Debra as Betsy's mother, there was a good chance his daughter would acquire the same personality. He could hope, at least.

Debra, he noticed, fed Betsy, ignoring her own salad.

"Aren't you going to eat?" he asked.

"I will as soon as Betsy is done."

He ate about half his hamburger and noticed that Debra was still tending to his daughter. "Let me feed her for a while so you can eat some of your salad."

"It won't take much longer."

"Debra, I want to feed Betsy now." He pulled his chair to the other side of Betsy's high chair and took the spoon from Debra's hand. "Eat your lunch, now."

Frustration shone in her eyes.

"I know you're upset with me, but you deserve to eat with the rest of us."

"This is part of my job," she said stubbornly, watching him as he fed Betsy as if she was sure he couldn't do it.

"Do you think Betsy didn't eat anything until you came?" he asked, hoping to tease her into better humor.

"She wasn't eating solid foods then. You might give her bites that are too big."

"You're right. You helped her change her diet and her sleeping habits. But that doesn't mean I can't help out. I don't want her to forget me."

"She won't."

"She might. Now eat some lunch or you're going to hurt their feelings." He nodded toward the kitchen. "They'll think you don't like their cooking."

He'd finally figured out that talking Debra into doing something for herself wouldn't work. But she'd do almost anything not to offend someone else. He didn't mind not eating for a while if it meant that Debra would eat. Now that he thought about it, she seemed thinner than when she first came. He'd have to keep an eye on that.

Lucy came out to check on them and saw John feeding Betsy when half his lunch was uneaten. Lucy never seemed to age. She wore a bit more cushion around the middle now in her fifties but she still had her natural red hair. And she wanted to mother the world. "What are you doing, John?"

"Feeding my little girl. Seems like she's got her daddy's appetite."

"Go finish your lunch. I got nothing to do and me and Betsy have always got along okay," Lucy said, pushing John out of his chair. "Get another chair from one of the other tables."

"I'll be glad to feed her, Lucy," Debra chimed in.

"Nonsense. John is right. You two need to nourish

yourselves. It takes a lot of energy to raise children. I should know. I raised six of them."

"Oh, my," Debra exclaimed. "Then you're an expert. I was a little afraid that John would give Betsy bites that were too big. But I know you'll do it right."

John rolled his eyes. "Thanks, dear wife, for all your support."

Debra ducked her head and he feared he'd been too hard on her. "Come on, Deb, I didn't mean to hurt your feelings."

"You didn't," she assured him, but she didn't look at him. She just started eating her salad again.

"Men aren't real good at realizing all that a woman has to do," Lucy said. "My hubby thought it was a simple matter."

"Does he understand now?" Debra asked.

"No, child, he died eight years ago. We still had three children at home. And he still thought they came out all dressed and ready for school."

Debra laughed. "I hope that's an exaggeration."

"Not much of one. But you don't have to worry about John, here. He and Bill did a good job taking care of Betsy. Say, someone said you're kin to Bill. Is that true?"

"Yes, I'm his niece."

"Then you're doubly welcome here. Bill's an old friend. And you make your husband bring you here on a Saturday night. That's our big night. Let us know and we'll save you a table."

"That's very sweet of you, Lucy, but cooking dinner is part of my job. I'm not sure John—"

"I think he would," John said at once, interrupting her. "You can put on your prettiest dress and we'll make an evening of it."

"We'll see," Debra said, ducking her head again.

What was wrong with the woman? He'd thought earlier she'd been upset with his teasing, but here he was offering her a night out on the town, what town there was, and she wouldn't even accept his invitation.

"I think she's full now, Lucy," Debra said. "Let's give her a cracker and see if she's satisfied. Then you can just enjoy visiting with us."

Betsy worked on a cracker, leaving the others time to eat. Debra asked Lucy several questions about her six children, and about the café. But when Lucy asked a few questions about Debra's life before she came to marry John, Debra avoided answering.

John got up to refill his Coke. Lucy jumped up. "I'll get that, John. How about you, Andy? Do you need more Coke?"

Andy looked at his mother. She shook her head.

"No, thank you," Andy said.

"My, you are such a gentleman, Andy. Your mama has done you proud."

Andy again looked at his mother. "Is that a good thing, Mommy?"

"Yes, sweetie, it is."

"Thank you," Andy said to Lucy.

Lucy beamed at the little boy. "He just makes you want to hug him, doesn't he?"

"Yeah," John agreed. "He's a great kid."

A few minutes later, they'd finished their meal and said goodbye to Baldy, Aggie and Lucy, promising to come again. But Debra didn't make a specific promise. John began to wonder if she had been pretending to enjoy herself at lunch.

"Didn't you like the café?" he asked as Debra backed the truck out of the parking space.

She turned to stare at him. "Didn't I say I liked it?"

"Yes, but you could've just said that because it was the nice thing to say."

"No, I really liked it."

"So why did you hedge about coming on a Saturday night?"

"Because I would embarrass you."

"How?"

"I don't have a dress to wear."

"Well, it's a good thing we're going shopping, then," John said.

"You can't buy me clothes."

"Sorry, Debra. I can buy you whatever I want. I'm your husband."

When they entered the general store, Debra said, "We'll meet you up front in a few minutes."

"Okay. I've got to talk to Charlie," John said.

Debra took Andy and Betsy to the children's section. "Andy, we're just getting Betsy's things today, because I don't have any money yet. Okay?"

"Okay, Mommy."

Debra thought he looked sad, but she didn't know what to do. Until she finished and sold a quilt, she wouldn't have money.

She picked out four outfits for Betsy and some diapers, then headed to the front of the store where the cash register was.

John was still talking to the owner. "You get everything you needed?" he asked.

"Yes," she said, putting the purchases on the counter.

John eyed the clothes, then without a word to her, turned to Charlie. "Can you find some jeans for Andy? He's growing fast."

When Charlie started back to the children's section, Debra whispered to John through clenched teeth. "I told you I'd buy him jeans later!"

"I'll buy them *now*!"

Debra stood there holding his baby, stiff as a board.

Charlie brought two pairs of jeans for them to choose between.

"We'll take both of them, Charlie. And maybe a couple of knit shirts." John walked back to the children's area, taking Andy with him.

Her son was very excited, but Debra didn't blame him. He was only a little boy.

When they came back with three shirts, John reached out to take Betsy. "Give me the baby and go pick out something nice for yourself."

"No, thank you," she said unemotionally.

"Deb, you're going to need clothes for church, if nothing else. It's important in this community to attend church."

"I'll figure out something," she muttered, determined not to give in.

John sighed. "Okay, this is it, Charlie."

After he paid, he took the bag and hobbled out the door, then held it for Debra and the children.

Once they were in the truck heading back home, he let loose. "I'm very angry with you, Debra! Why can't you just take the clothes?"

"I tried to explain to you that I need to pay for what we buy," she said stonily.

"How are you going to earn that money? You're working like a slave for me. You don't have time for another job. And as hard as you work, I don't think taking a dress or two should be a problem. You've earned more than that."

She said nothing.

"So, how are you going to go to church Sunday? Explain that to me!"

She still said nothing.

He huffed and crossed his arms over his chest. "I hope you don't teach the kids to be this stubborn."

They were silent for the rest of the drive. When they got home, she took the children into the house.

John grabbed the bag and hurried after her.

"Are you going to let Andy keep the clothes? I hope you don't intend—"

She turned to face him. "Of course I am, John. I would never be cruel to my child. And I'll pay you back what they cost."

John immediately ripped the tags off the clothes, hoping that would stop her from knowing what he'd paid.

"Don't be so childish, John," she said sternly. Then, in a much softer voice, she told her son, "It's time for your nap, Andy."

"Aw, Mommy," he began, but his mother's stern look made him change his mind. He turned to John. "Thank you for my new jeans and shirts."

"You're welcome, Andy."

"Now, upstairs to your room. I'm going to put Betsy down. Then I'll come check on you," Debra said with a warm smile for her son.

He trudged up the stairs ahead of her and Betsy.

"Hey, what about me?" John called.

"You should probably rest, also. I'm sure walking with the cast is tiring." She kept on going up the stairs.

Determined not to do what she'd said, he settled in front of the television, keeping the sound low so as not to distract Andy. He had almost fallen asleep when he heard Debra on the stairs. He sat up a little straighter and pretended to be alert and interested in the show.

"You decided not to rest?"

"I don't need a nap. I'm a little older than Andy!"

"I would hope so. But you haven't been up much since you hurt your leg."

"I can manage. Now, tomorrow I might need some rest."

Debra paused and looked at him. "Why would you need rest tomorrow and not today?"

"Because it's time I got back in the saddle," he said nonchalantly.

Debra whirled around to stare at him. "It's time you did what?"

"Got back in the saddle again."

"So, you mean you're going to ride for an hour or so to get used to it again?"

"No, I mean I'll be riding out in the morning with all the others."

CHAPTER NINE

DEBRA threw things around in the kitchen, making as much racket as she could. Why should she care if the man damaged his leg again? She didn't! she assured herself. It would be foolish to care about a man who was dumping her at the end of the summer. But the idea of his riding out in the morning was beyond stupid!

"Debra?" John said from the doorway, as if afraid to enter his own kitchen.

"Yes?"

"Honey, I didn't mean to upset you, but I need to be out there working. Now that there are five of us, I think we'll be able to handle all the work, thanks to your idea about selling the Escalade. That's all I'm thinking of."

"Making more money isn't what's important! You need to ease back into the job. If you're exhausted, you'll make mistakes that might even endanger the other men. Why don't you just ride out a half day? Then you can come in, have lunch and rest."

"If I did that, I'd have to bring everyone in for lunch. When you're the boss, you don't pamper yourself and no one else!"

"No one else broke his leg!"

"That's true, but—"

"Oh, just get out of my kitchen! *I* have work to do!"

Debra already had meat marinating in the fridge for dinner. Now she wanted to bake a peach cobbler, one of her favorite recipes. Anything to keep busy. She should be glad John was going out in the morning. Things would be back to normal. That was what she wanted, wasn't it?

She didn't want to answer that question. Was she irritated with John because he'd bought the clothes for her son? Was she mad because he'd almost made a scene about buying her a dress? No, she was just worried about the crazy man, which was ridiculous.

After protesting about the dress, she now hated to admit she had a problem. Today was Wednesday, giving her four days to find something to wear to church on Sunday.

John's mind had apparently been running along the same lines, because as he came into the kitchen again he said, "About your clothes situation... Maybe you could look through Elizabeth's closet and find something to wear. I mean, I think you're about the same size. No point in all those clothes just hanging there."

"A woman named Adele called about the Westlake

Auxiliary's fair next month. She wanted you to sell your wife's clothes. She said you could earn a lot of money."

"Why don't you take what you want, and we'll donate the rest of them to charity? It's time I cleaned out her closet, anyway. Can you do that for me? And don't worry about anyone around here having seen the clothes on her. She didn't hang out in Westlake, and she never went to church with me."

His bitter words made her want to give him a hug or soothe his brow, or something silly like that. John had been through a hard time with his first wife. He must be quite disillusioned. No wonder he'd been so rude to her in the beginning.

"I'll take care of it," she promised, keeping her head down and continuing to prepare the dough for the cobbler.

With a deep sigh, he said, "Thanks, I appreciate it." Then he went back into the living room and sat down in front of the television.

Debra warned herself about feeling too sorry for John. After all, her life hadn't been a picnic, either. Even though she'd only turned twenty-two, she felt like a hundred on some days.

With stiffened resolve not to feel sorry for herself or John, she concentrated on the cobblers. Finally, pleased with the lattice, she slid them into the oven, when she heard John's voice behind her.

"Those look good."

"Thank you. Are you watching television?"

"There's only stupid stuff on. It's either the soaps or news shows. I can't figure out which one is worse."

"You could try closing your eyes and resting," she suggested.

"I don't want to fall asleep! That's why I got up."

Hardheaded to the bitter end. "I'd be happy to wake you up before the men come in."

"No, thanks. I'll go check the freezer and make sure we have some vanilla ice cream to go on top of those cobblers. The men will love those."

She was grateful for the respite. Back in Kansas City, she'd worked with others in the kitchen in her old job, but John in her kitchen was way too distracting.

"We've got plenty of vanilla ice cream," he said as he came back. "Maybe too much—if that's possible."

"Well, I'll try not to resort to ice cream on a regular basis."

"Not to worry. The men have been raving about your cooking since the first night. As we rode in each evening, they would speculate on what was for dinner."

"They would? I didn't know that. They've certainly been complimentary, which I appreciated, but I didn't know—"

John looked down at his feet. "I guess I forgot to tell you you were doing a bang-up job. I was worried about you getting the wrong idea if I said too much."

It took her a moment to understand what he was

saying. "The wrong— Oh, no, I wouldn't. I mean, I understand what I'm doing here."

John stared at Debra. He wanted to ask if she was willing to change her job description to include the true wifely duties, but somehow he didn't think she was ready yet.

He was. Much to his surprise, the idea of sharing his bedroom with Debra was beginning to dominate his thoughts. He looked at her again. Then he frowned. She was beginning to look almost frail. What was going on?

Remembering his vow to watch her eating habits, he sat down at the table. "What are you doing now?"

"I'm getting out the silverware so I can set the table."

"But you've got time till the guys get in."

"Setting the table early won't hurt anything."

"I'll do it," he said, standing to take the silverware from her. But she pulled away.

"Don't you ever sit down and rest?"

"Of course I do. Once the kitchen is clean, I have the evening free." She briskly set about peeling potatoes and making a salad. After a few moments of feeling his eyes boring into her back, she turned around. "John, you need to go find something to do. You're driving me crazy."

"Why?"

"Because you're staring at me. What about the paperwork Bill told me about? He said you were behind in that."

"I guess I could go work on it." He stood. "Do you have any cookies? I could use a snack."

In exasperation, she fixed him a plate of cookies and poured him a glass of milk.

"I haven't drunk so much milk since I was a teenager," he commented.

She reached out to take the glass of milk and he quickly moved out of her reach. "No, I was just commenting, not complaining. It goes good with the cookies."

"Fine. Then go work on your papers and enjoy your snack."

John smiled as he left the kitchen. So his stare bothered her? Good. He wanted to bother her, to disturb her. To have her thinking about him.

That was the first step in getting her to be his wife— in every sense of the word.

The next morning, Debra served breakfast to the men as usual, and was feeding cereal to Betsy, who was unusually fussy. Between bites, John lectured her. "Remember how Lucy said yesterday that moms need to have energy for the kids? Well, it takes food for you to get that energy."

"I'll have time to eat later, John. I'm not riding out today," she said, glaring at him.

"Come on, Debra, I can't hurt myself with my leg in a cast."

"Whatever." She ignored him for the remainder of the meal.

Later, as the men cleared out, she gave them their

lunches as they left. She was surprised when John, the last in line, reached out for his.

"You're taking your lunch today?" she asked. She always fixed it in case he changed his mind. When he didn't take it, she and the kids ate it for their noon meal.

"Yes, I am. I thought I might really need it today."

"Good." She handed it to him, expecting him to follow the others out the door. He did—but only after kissing her goodbye. Shock, then pleasure ran through her. Then panic. She wasn't supposed to want him. It was inappropriate. He was going to fire her as soon as he could.

"He needn't think he can have his way with me!" she muttered to herself after he left.

"What's the matter, Mommy?" Andy asked. "Are you unhappy with John?"

"No, sweetie. I'm just trying to take care of everything."

Next time, she reminded herself, she'd have to remember how astute and perceptive her three-year-old was. "Finish your breakfast now, son."

"John said you should eat breakfast, too," Andy said, watching her.

She rolled her eyes. Then she picked up a piece of bacon and chewed on it. "I'm eating, see?" Now she had two males watching after her.

Maybe Andy was spending too much time with adults, she thought.

She wished she knew someone with a child Andy's age. Maybe if they went to church as John said, she could meet another mother and they could work out some playtime for the children.

After Betsy and Andy were finished, she took the baby and her playpen into John's bedroom.

"What are you doing, Mommy?" Andy asked, coming in after her.

"I'm cleaning up John's bedroom. Then I have to clean out his wife's closet."

"I thought you were his wife."

"I'm his second wife, honey. I meant Betsy's mother."

"Her clothes are still here?"

"Yes. John said I could wear any of them I want."

"Oh. Can I watch television in here with you and Betsy?"

"Okay, honey. Let me get his sheets off the bed."

Once she'd put them in the laundry, she dusted his room and cleaned the bathroom. Then she opened the closet door where Elizabeth's clothes were hanging. It was like having an exclusive store where you were the only customer. Debra found a couple of pair of jeans. They were designer, but still practical enough. There were some blouses—silk, of course.

Most of the clothes were too flashy for her but she did find two suits that she could wear to church.

All in all, though she doubled the size of her wardrobe, she had only taken less than a tenth of Elizabeth's wardrobe. But she agreed with Adele about selling the clothes at the fair. After all, John could use the money.

"Mommy?"

"Yes, sweetie?" she asked.

"How many ladies wore all those clothes?"

"Only one," she said with a wry grin.

"Wow! That's a lot of clothes."

Her son was right, of course. But some of them were never worn at all. The khaki suit, for instance, which still had the tags attached.

After she carried all the clothes to an empty closet in Betsy's room, she put the children down for a nap and settled herself at the kitchen table to quilt. Last night she'd stayed up too late sewing. She couldn't do that often, despite her hope to have four quilts ready to sell at the fair.

An opportunity to sell what she made wouldn't come along often.

With steely determination, she worked until it was time to fix dinner.

She stretched and poured herself a cup of coffee, hoping the caffeine would help her.

She moved about the kitchen on autopilot, preparing dinner. Then she heard Betsy stirring. She hurried up the stairs to collect her, changed her diaper, and she opened Andy's bedroom door. He was quietly playing with a couple of small trucks John had given him.

"Are you ready to get up, sweetie?"

"Yes, Mommy. I tried to be quiet so I wouldn't wake Betsy."

"You didn't. It was time for her to get up. Come on, let's go to the kitchen."

Just as they reached the bottom of the stairs, they heard the back door open. Debra ran toward the door. "Hello? What's wrong?"

"Now, Debra, it's no big deal," Bill said. "I just thought John had been in the saddle long enough. Is it okay if he rests here on the sofa until dinner?"

"Of course, Uncle Bill. Andy, go get the two pillows on John's bed for me."

Andy ran to John's bedroom.

"Don't say anything, Debra. I should've been able to finish out the day," John said, his teeth set.

"Of course, you should've, Superman." She went to the kitchen and poured him a cup of hot coffee. When she added some cookies on a saucer, she brought them back to the living room. John was shoving pillows behind his back on the sofa.

"Here," Debra said, putting the cup and plate on the big coffee table that could be reached from all three sofas. Andy eyed John's cookies. Debra put down a napkin with cookies on it for Andy. "Don't eat too many, sweetie. You have to eat your dinner in an hour or two."

"Yes, ma'am, Mommy," Andy said, a happy smile on his face.

"Aren't you going to tell me not to eat too much?" John asked.

"No, you need all the calories you can get," she said, as if she didn't care. But she did. In fact, over time she'd come to realize she ached for him. He'd tried to do what he thought was right. He truly was a good man.

Every once in a while, when she paused, she would think about how wonderful it would be if they were truly married. Oh, she knew legally they were. But she dreamed of being John's wife, of having the right to touch him when she wanted. And where she wanted.

This was one of those times, and she reveled in her fantasies.

After Debra was back in the kitchen, Andy leaned over and whispered, "Is Mommy mad at you?"

"Yeah, I guess so," John replied.

"What did you do?" the boy managed to ask through a mouthful of cookie.

"She said I should only work a half day but I insisted on working a whole day."

Andy nodded. "My mom is always right." He reached across the sofa and patted John on his good leg. "It's okay, though. She doesn't stay mad for long. No matter what I do, she always gives me a hug and a kiss before I go to bed."

John couldn't help but grin. "I'm not sure she'll do that for me, Andy. But thanks, anyway."

Unbidden, images of Debra leaning down to tuck him in snuck into his mind's eye. The bedroom was dark…she wore her robe, open a bit as she leaned over him, giving him a glance of her creamy white skin…and she smelled that vanilla smell that he loved about her….

Oh, yeah. He could hardly wait till bedtime.

CHAPTER TEN

DEBRA was working on her quilt after dinner that night when John once again distracted her.

"There's a good show on television. Want to come watch it with me?"

"No, thank you. I'm busy."

"Do you ever watch television?"

"Not really." She kept her head and down and continued to work.

She almost jumped out of her skin when she felt his hands on her shoulders. "What in heaven's name are you doing?"

"Hey, take it easy, Deb. I just thought I'd massage your shoulders a little. They looked stiff."

She felt like she was going to explode. They never touched each other, except in an emergency. His idea of massaging her shoulders wasn't going to ease her tension. "John, is there something I need to do? Did I forget anything?"

"No, nothing. Dinner was great tonight. I could eat another piece of cake, if there's any left over."

She shoved her chair back to rise.

"No, no, there's not need for you to get it. I can do it. Can I cut you a piece, too?"

"No, thank you. I'm fine."

"How much dinner did you eat?"

"Why are you asking me that?"

"I don't think you're eating enough. I bet I could put my hands around your waist and they'd meet."

She felt herself shrink back from him. "Let's not try."

"Then let me cut you a piece of cake."

"Fine," she agreed. "Cut me a piece of cake."

A couple of minutes later, he put a saucer with a big piece of cake on it beside her. "Do you want milk?"

"No, thank you."

"I'm going to have milk. I'll just pour you a small glass." Then he set a glass down beside her.

She looked up, expecting to see him disappearing into the other room. Instead, he sat down across from her. "What are you doing?" she asked. She was already tired and she needed to get a lot of work done tonight. She mustn't forget that she was only here for a little while. But John seemed to be playing a dangerous game. One that she couldn't afford to play.

"I'm having my snack."

"What about the good television show you were talking about?"

"It's not that good. I'd rather talk to you."

"John, how dense can you be? I'm working! I don't want to chat with you. I have work I have to get done!"

"I got that, but I don't understand why," John said, staring at her. "Can you tell me why it's so important?"

"Yes. I'm making the quilts so I can sell them at the fair next month. That way I can earn some money."

"Honey, if you need money, all you have to do is ask. You've more than earned it."

"No, thank you. Now go away and leave me alone."

He picked up his cup and dish and walked out of the kitchen without another word.

As Debra stared after him, her eyes filled with tears. She couldn't remember the last time she'd cried, but she did now.

Today she'd finally admitted to herself that she was coming to care for the man. Little good it did her! Their marriage had been doomed from the start. She remembered that day in the little church, how she'd had cross words with her uncle and how John had been so cross with her.

The tears flowed harder, unchecked down her cheeks and onto her shirt. She cried because she cared for him. Because she wanted him.

And because she could never have him.

So why did he keep torturing her?

John got up early the next morning. The kitchen light was the only one on in the house. He wondered if perhaps Debra had fallen asleep at the table last night and never gone to bed.

When he reached the kitchen, he discovered Debra was up preparing breakfast. He cleared his throat, just to let her know she wasn't alone. She spun around. "John! What are you doing up so early?"

"I was afraid you might not be able to get up. Need any help?"

She didn't appear grateful. She turned her back and kept mixing the pancake batter. "No, thank you."

"Debra, I'm worried about you. I want you to relax a little, enjoy life." He wanted her to feel like she was at home, her home. To become a part of his home.

She set the pancake batter aside and put on the coffee. "Coffee will be ready in a few minutes."

"Okay."

Then she put a large skillet on the stovetop and began frying the breakfast meats.

John noticed that she had already made the lunches. "Debra, when did you get up this morning?"

"A half hour ago."

"Is that all?" He checked his watch. It was a quarter of six. The men would be there in fifteen minutes. "You work fast."

"Yes, it's all routine."

Then she broke eggs into a bowl.

"We get scrambled eggs, too?"

"Yes. Some of the men like them."

"I liked them. In fact, I haven't found anything you make that I don't like."

"Thank you."

"By the way, I have a favor to ask of you."

Debra turned to stare at him. "Are you serious?"

"Yeah. They're going to deliver a washer and dryer to go in the bunkhouse this afternoon. Can you show them where to put it and make sure it all works before you let them go? And they're delivering a television for the bunkhouse, too."

Debra stared at him. "Why? What are you doing?"

"I thought I'd take a little work off your shoulders. The men can all do their own laundry. There's no need for you to do it."

"But, I—"

He stopped her. "I don't want you to get worn-out. You need to get more sleep and eat more."

"Are you telling me I'm not doing my job?"

"Hell, no! You're doing it better than any two people could. But I didn't mean for you to work so hard. I'm just trying to improve your quality of life a little. Is that okay?"

"The men will think I've been complaining."

"No, they won't. I'll tell them. I'll take the blame. I'm too jealous to have my wife tired because she's folding some other guy's underwear."

"That's ridiculous. They'll never believe that!"

"I don't know why not. It's the truth."

"No, it's not!"

He gripped her shoulders. "I want all your attention focused on me and Betsy. That's normal. It's the other way that isn't." Then he kissed her.

Debra's first thought was he was getting very good at kissing her. Then she wondered why he was kissing her. She shoved him back. "Stop that!"

"Why? I liked it." He lowered his head again.

"Something's burning!" She spun around and speared a piece of ham that had burnt to a crisp.

"Debra," he began, but she stopped him.

"I have to have breakfast on the table in ten minutes. Why don't you go get the kids?"

John couldn't very well refuse to do that now, not after he'd told her he was there to help her. He went upstairs, slowly and dejectedly, muttering to himself, "Why didn't I tell her I wanted to be alone with her and kiss her?"

Debra closed her eyes for only a moment after John left the kitchen. She had to make sure he stopped the kissing. It was too much.

Then, after looking at her watch, she continued preparing breakfast before the men arrived.

She wondered how they would take the announcement that they were to do their own laundry. As she cut out biscuits and put them in a pan, she hoped they wouldn't think they'd caused her too much trouble. They were appreciative of what she did.

Was John buying them a television so they wouldn't hang out in the living room here? And where was he getting all this money? Why hadn't he already hired a housekeeper? Suddenly, she realized maybe she didn't have as much time here as she'd thought.

Just then, John came back into the kitchen with Betsy. She reached out a hand for Debra and called, "Ma-ma!"

"Good morning, sweetie," Debra said, leaning over to give her a kiss.

John put her in her high chair. "Andy will be down in a minute. He's such a good kid."

"Thank you." She gave John a baby cup of milk for Betsy. "Why don't you start her with this while I get her cereal?"

John looked surprised. "A cup? No bottle?"

Over her shoulder Debra replied, "She's got to learn, John. By one, she should be off the bottle completely."

"That makes sense, then. Hey, look! She can drink all by herself." Betsy had taken the handles in her hands...and proceeded to spill the milk all over her tray.

Debra hurried over with a dry cloth. "Sometimes she misses her mouth. It's better if you guide her a little."

"Ah, I see. Well, Betsy, you've got a lot to learn, but so do I. I guess we can learn together."

Just then, the cowboys began filing in. They each greeted Debra. Since it was Thursday, Darrell told her he'd left his laundry bag in the laundry room.

Before John could say anything, Debra assured Darrell he'd have his laundry done when he got in that evening.

"But then that's the end of that service," John said. "Debra is wearing herself out taking care of all of us. So I'm having a new washer and dryer delivered to the bunkhouse today, so you can do your own laundry."

All of the men agreed, especially when John told them he had bought them a big television, too. "That way, you can watch television while you fold your own laundry."

While the men all laughed, Andy padded into the room. He slipped into his seat and Debra greeted him with a kiss. Then she made him pancakes, as she'd done the others. "Andy, you need to eat a little bit of eggs, too, please."

"Aw, Mom," he protested.

"Son, you have to do as your mom says. It's what a cowboy does," John told him, all serious.

Andy frowned. "Really?"

"Ask any of them," John said, motioning to the others at the table. To a man, they all assured Andy they obeyed their mamas.

Debra had trouble hiding her smile. She didn't believe it was true, but if it got her son to follow orders, she figured it was a good thing. She looked up and her gaze met John's.

There was an intimacy in his gaze, as if they shared secrets, like some couples who had lived together a long time. What a ridiculous thought. The longest she'd be on the ranch was six months. She hurriedly looked away.

When the men finished and started filing out, she passed out their lunches. Again, John held back, waiting for the others to leave. When he approached her, Debra took a step back and held out his lunch at arm's length.

John stood there, but it was Andy who asked the question. "What's wrong, Mommy? Don't you want John to kiss you goodbye like yesterday? That's what mommys and daddys do. I saw it on TV!"

John smiled at the boy's comment, but his eyes never left Debra's. Neither did hers leave his. He stepped closer, took his lunch and, when she thought she'd never breathe again, kissed her goodbye.

When she heard the door shut behind her, Debra went to her son. "You, little man," she said, ruffling his shaggy hair, "watch too much TV."

"That was a nice thing you did," Bill said as John rode up beside him.

"What are you talking about?"

"Getting us those machines so we can do our own laundry. That's a big load off Debra's back. I bet she was real grateful," Bill added with a suggestive laugh.

"No, she wasn't."

Bill frowned. "Really? Why? It can't be because she liked doing our dirty work."

"She acted like I was saying she couldn't do her job properly." John was silent for a moment. Then he said, "She does the work of at least two women and never complains. And now she's staying up too late at night making a quilt so she can sell it and make money. I tried to get her to tell me what she needed money for, but she wouldn't. Do you know what's going on?"

"She told me she was quilting. My mother taught her. I thought she was doing it because she liked it so much."

"Think, Bill, after all the cooking and cleaning she does, the child care for two children, the laundry, do you really think she has time left over for a hobby? I'd like her to be able to get out some, to have some leisure time."

"That'd be nice," Bill said. "But she seems all right."

"You don't think she's lost weight?"

"Maybe a little, but she's okay."

"I'm worried about her."

"Well, that's your job, and I'm glad you're doing it. You didn't take to her right away, did you?"

"Damn it, Bill, you know I didn't want to marry. But Debra was everything and more that you said she was. But we both shortchanged her on the wedding. She didn't even get flowers!"

"Won't be much to tell your kids about, will it?"

"If we ever have any."

"I don't see why you wouldn't, if you want 'em."

"Maybe the fact that we don't share the same bedroom, much less the same bed!"

"Still?"

"Hell, Bill, she's only been here a couple of weeks.

Don't you think I should let her adjust? Figure out if she even likes me? I spent so much money and time to give Elizabeth the wedding she wanted, and she threw it all away. And she didn't do anything to deserve it, either. But Debra…"

His eyes stared off in the distance as he considered his second wife. She was the complete opposite of his first wife, for which he gave thanks. But he was greedy and wanted more.

He wanted to be her real husband, to care for her and their two kids. To make more children. To leave a legacy that could continue for generations.

He wanted to feel her in the bed beside him. To snuggle up to her on cold nights…or hot nights, he thought with a grin. He wanted to share the hard times and the good times with Debra.

"What are you thinking about, boy? Is it X-rated?"

John's cheeks flushed. "Why would you think that?"

"Something on your face, I guess. Come on, we've got to check the herd, make sure none of the mama cows are down." They directed the men to ride the pasture looking for any cows in distress. "If you need help, fire a shot in the air."

They spread out to search the pasture. John had to pay attention, to be alert, so he could lend assistance if it was needed. He noted several calves obviously born the night before. Then he found a cow down and took his chains out of the saddlebag in case he needed to pull the calf. It could mean the difference between life and death for the calf and possibly the mother.

It was clear this birth wasn't going easy. He managed to attach the chains to the calf's back legs and pulled the calf out of her mother. It took the calf a moment to adjust and John cleared out its nostrils. But it started breathing and a couple of minutes later, it stood on its own, though it was still a little wobbly.

John remounted and looked for another cow in trouble to repeat the process again.

They rode the pasture until it was almost dark. Then they gathered and rode together back to the barn, knowing Debra would have a great meal fixed for them. When John came in the house, while the others went to shower, he could smell the delicious aromas. His stomach growled.

Debra had left him his clean clothes on the bench where he always sat down to pull off his boots. He stripped and took his shower. Then he quickly dressed in clean clothes. He thought back to those days when he and the men would drag in after dark and have to make supper. It's a wonder they didn't poison each other.

He headed for the kitchen and was greeted by Andy and Betsy. He kissed and hugged both of them. Debra had her back to him and she didn't turn around. He walked up to her and slid his arms around her, feeling her jump in surprise. He kissed her cheek, since he couldn't reach her lips.

"How was your day?" he asked as he released her.

"Fine! It was fine. How was your day?"

"Good. We've got a lot of new calves."

"I want to see them!" Andy called out.

John poured himself a cup of coffee and sat down at the table. "We'll arrange a time when I can take you out, Andy. You won't mind riding on my horse with me, will you?"

"No, I want to!" Andy said excitedly.

"He's too young, John."

Both John and Andy looked at Debra in surprise. John put his hand on Andy's shoulder to keep him quiet. "I promise my horse is safe, Debra. She's really well trained and I wouldn't let her run."

"She's safe unless she sees a snake!"

"Accidents happen, Debra, but I don't think lightning strikes twice in the same place."

"I don't think it's a good idea," Debra persisted.

"Mommy, other boys get to ride horses!" Andy protested.

"Not three-year-old boys, Andy."

"When do you turn four, Andy?" John asked.

"I don't know. When do I have my birthday, Mommy?"

"In October, sweetie, and that's a long time away."

"We'll try to persuade your mommy before your birthday, but if we can't, then on your birthday, you'll get to go riding for sure!"

"Yeah!" Andy cheered. Something about his mother made him ask, "Right, Mommy?"

"Right, sweetie...if we're still here."

CHAPTER ELEVEN

"WHAT are you talking about, Debra?" John demanded, standing to gain her attention.

The back door opened just then and John knew he'd lost his chance to ask her anything unless he wanted to do so in front of his men. He'd have to wait until after dinner.

"Hey, Debra, I swear we could smell your cooking all the way from the bunkhouse," Mikey said as he sat down, ignoring the tension in the room.

"I hope it was appetizing, Mikey," Debra said with a smile.

John glowered at her. She didn't offer him those warm smiles.

"Of course it was," Jess said, beaming at Debra, who also returned his smile.

Damn! Did she like everyone better than him?

"Debra, what are we having tonight?" he asked, watching her closely.

She rattled off the menu without ever looking at him.

John sought for another question, but it was Bill who asked, "What's for dessert, honey?"

Again, she smiled at Bill as she answered. John was apparently the only one whom she disliked.

John sat through dinner, frustration almost overruling his appetite. Almost. But he also remembered he wanted to see how much Debra ate. She served, she fed Betsy, she supervised Andy. But she never took a bite herself. After dinner, there was the cleanup and she had to get the kids to bed.

"I'll give Betsy her bottle tonight," John offered. "I can do that just as well with a cast as I can with two good legs."

Debra looked surprised. "I can do it."

"No, I'll feed Betsy and you bathe Andy. That will get them in bed sooner."

"I'll just go change her diaper—"

"I can do that, Debra. You can't take everything on your shoulders."

"Fine!" She angrily went up the stairs with Andy.

With a wry grin, he carried his daughter upstairs to her room and changed her diaper. Then they came back down, and he warmed up her bottle and settled on one of the leather sofas in front of the big television. He remembered the nights when he'd tried to feed Betsy before he ate his dinner, miserable and exhausted.

Tonight, he'd been well-fed and was wearing clean clothes, holding his little girl against him. Life was good.

But he still needed to discover what Debra had meant about not being there next October.

He tried discussing it with Betsy, but she had nothing to say on the subject. She just fluttered her eyelashes at him, and he was satisfied. In a soft voice, he told his little girl about his day, describing the baby calves, telling her how they wobbled when they tried to walk. Her gaze remained fixed on his lips as she took her bottle.

Debra came down the stairs before Betsy finished. "Shall I take over for you?" she asked.

"No, thanks. It won't take much longer."

She walked into the kitchen and he could hear her moving around, cleaning up after supper. He'd intended to talk to her about eating before she put everything away. Maybe she was eating now, but he'd never know unless Betsy hurried up. Only a couple of minutes later, the milk was gone and Betsy was falling asleep.

He put his daughter to bed, then he hurried back down, as much as his cast would allow him, to reach the kitchen. Debra was closing the dishwasher and starting it.

"Debra, did you eat?"

She turned around and glowered at him. "Yes."

"What did you eat?"

"Different things. I nibbled and tasted as I prepared dinner."

"That's not sitting down and eating a meal. You're losing weight. Didn't Tom's words do anything for you?"

"I'm strong enough to do my job, John. Tell me if you think I'm slacking off somewhere and I'll take care of it!"

"It's not that you're not doing everything and more than I ask, Debra. I'm concerned with your health."

"I don't need you to guard my health. I'm an adult. I can take care of myself."

"Okay. I'll change subjects. What did you mean when you said, 'If we're here in October.' Why wouldn't you be here? How can you say something that will upset Andy, make him not feel settled?"

"Andy will be okay. He knows I'll take care of him."

"So tell me what you mean."

"Nothing. Life changes. I don't know what it will hold."

"Debra, you're not telling me something." He was learning to read her body language even more than he understood her words. And he sensed that there was a reason for those words.

"You know everything I know, and neither of us can read the future. Now I have work to do, if you'll excuse me."

"You're going to quilt again?"

"Yes, unless you have something you need me to do."

"How about I need you to keep me company and watch a movie with me?"

"No, thank you. I prefer quilting."

John limped out of the kitchen, depressed and upset. Something was wrong, and she wasn't willing to talk to him about it. Maybe he could press Bill and get him to talk to her. But Bill didn't seem much in tune with his niece.

Another thought struck him. If she knew she could sell her quilts whenever she made one and didn't have to have them ready for the fair, some of the pressure might disappear. He'd have to call Charlie in the morning and ask him if he needed anything like that to sell in the store.

He'd have to come up with a reason for staying in in the morning until Charlie opened the store. He could fake soreness. She'd easily believe that. She'd been warning him about it ever since he got his cast on.

With a plan in mind, he relaxed and watched television…and fell asleep.

When he woke up, it was after midnight and Debra was still in the kitchen running that blasted sewing machine. He pushed up off the couch and limped to the kitchen door. "Debra, don't you think you need to go to bed?"

She jumped. "What time is it?"

"Almost one o'clock," he said, wondering if she'd pay attention. She seemed rather out of it.

"Oh, I didn't know. I'll put everything away and go up to bed." Then she looked up. "What are you doing up this late?"

He grinned. "I fell asleep on the sofa around eight-thirty. I just woke up."

"Oh."

He stepped forward. "Let me put the sewing machine away for you," he said, putting his hand on the handle of the case as she slid the machine in it.

"I can do that."

"I know you can, but let me help just this once."

She looked at him warily, but she finally agreed.

"Why don't you sleep in in the morning and I'll cook breakfast for the others?" he suggested.

"Absolutely not! That's my job," she said firmly.

"It's not like you're going to get fired if you take a day off, Debra."

"I'll be up at my regular time." Then she marched up the stairs as if she were climbing Mount Everest.

John stood at the bottom of the stairs, wishing she'd gone straight into his room and he could spoil her and make her relax and feel better, stronger. Why hadn't he found Debra first and not Elizabeth? She was exactly what he'd wanted in a wife, but years ago she wasn't around when he'd just gotten over his father's death and was looking for a connection with someone. He'd made that connection—or at least he thought he did— at a rodeo in Cheyenne where he'd met Elizabeth. The beautiful woman hadn't realized that watching cowboys was a far cry from living among them.

Debra, though, was the woman any man in his right mind would choose. But he had first dibs, and he intended to let her know that. She wouldn't be going anywhere before next October unless it was on a honeymoon with him.

Again John got up early the next morning. Debra wasn't surprised. She knew he didn't trust her to do her job. She was determined to prove him wrong. She'd catch up on her sleep this afternoon, while the kids were in bed.

She filled a mug of coffee for him and put it on the table in front of his usual seat.

"I could've gotten that."

"No need," she assured him. She even added a smile, though it was an effort this morning. She must be coming down with something. But it wouldn't be the first time she'd worked through a case of the flu.

By the time the men arrived, she had everything on the table except the second batch of biscuits. She liked to put it in the oven as the men arrived. Then, halfway through breakfast, they'd have hot biscuits to replace the others that were usually eaten by then.

She was feeding Betsy, proud of herself for managing everything as if she'd had eight hours of sleep instead of four. She knew she hadn't been getting enough sleep, but there was so little time. She'd almost finished the second quilt. If she hurried, she might finish four before the fair.

"Don't grab the spoon, Betsy," Debra ordered as she fed the little girl. Betsy was growing so quickly, and learning new things every day.

The buzzer went off on the oven. Debra jumped up from her seat to get the hot biscuits. Suddenly the world turned upside down and she fell to the floor, silent.

John leaped from his chair but Bill was beside Debra while he was on the other side of the table. He may have gotten to her second, but he took charge as he gathered her up from Bill. "Bill, call Doc and see if he'll come out. Jess, you take care of Betsy. Mikey, you've got Andy, and Darrell, you get the biscuits out of the oven."

Then he hurried down the hall to his bedroom. He laid her gently on his bed. He rushed into the bathroom to wet a cloth. As he came back to the bed, her eyelids fluttered and she tried to sit up.

"Lie back down," he ordered at once.

"Wh-what am I doing in here?"

She'd actually followed his orders. That pleased him. "You passed out when you jumped up to get the biscuits out of the oven."

She pushed herself up again.

"No way. Lie back down. Darrell got the biscuits out."

"But Betsy—"

"Jess is taking care of her."

"Andy—"

"Mikey."

"But there's nothing wrong with me."

"I think there is, and Bill is calling the doctor to come see. Until he gets here, you don't leave this bed."

"But it's not my bed!"

Damn. He'd hoped she wouldn't notice.

"I didn't want to try carrying you upstairs with my leg."

"I'll go sit on the sofa and wait for the doctor." She paused before she asked, "Will he really make a house call? I mean, I don't want him to go to any trouble. I may have a touch of the flu, but I don't need a doctor for that."

Again, she started to get up. He put his hand on her shoulder. "Honey, you have to stay down until Tom figures out what's wrong." He remembered that she only did things for others, not herself. "What if you'd passed out carrying Betsy?"

Her immediate in-drawn breath told him she recognized the problem. She didn't rise up again. "Can—can Andy come in and see me? I know he's worried."

"Sure. If you promise not to move, I'll go get him."

After she nodded, he hurried back to the kitchen. "Andy, your mom is awake. She thought you might want to come see her so you wouldn't worry."

"Yes, please," Andy said.

John was amazed he still minded his manners. Reaching for the little boy's hand, he led him down the hall.

"But Mommy's room is upstairs," Andy pointed out.

"Yes, but don't mention that. It would make Mommy feel bad because she's borrowing my bed."

"Oh."

They went into the bedroom and Debra was lying

curled up on her side. "Andy!" she said, reaching for him. "Are you all right?"

"Sure I am, Mommy. I didn't fall. You did."

Bill walked into the room. "Doc's on his way."

"I don't think he should make the trip out here just for me. I promise I just have a touch of the flu."

Bill patted her shoulder. "I think John is right. You need to make sure you're all right. You could hurt yourself real bad."

"How is Betsy?" Debra asked.

John sighed. "You're not going to be happy until everyone is in here, are you? I'll go get Betsy. Bill, you'd better take the guys and get out there. I'll come if Deb is all right."

"Bill, the lunches are on the cabinet waiting for you," Debra called as Bill left the room.

"Stay down," John said, before leaving to go get Betsy.

He had a pretty good idea about what was wrong with Debra, but he wanted the doctor to tell her. She wouldn't listen to him.

Betsy was in her high chair, fussing at Jess. John could hear her as he got to the kitchen. "What are you doing to my child, Jess?"

"Trying to feed her, but she's trying to tell me something. I think she's upset 'cause you and Debra aren't here."

Betsy was waving at her daddy and calling to him. He came over and picked her up. "It's okay, Betsy. You should thank Jess, but I guess we'll have to wait a while before you can do that." He kissed Betsy's cheek. "But I'll say thank you, Jess. I appreciate all of you pitching in. Darrell, did you turn off the oven?"

"Yes, I did." He dropped his gaze. "And we ate most of the biscuits. We saved you two."

"That's not a problem. I'm going to stay here with Debra and the babies until the doctor gets here and can tell us what's wrong."

"We'll cover for you, boy. Just take care of Debbie," Bill said as he herded his depleted crew out the door.

John put his lunch in the fridge and then took Betsy to his bedroom. As soon as she saw Debra, Betsy began reaching toward her, calling, "Ma-ma."

Debra raised up and John looked at her. "You promised to stay down."

"I just wanted to reassure Betsy," she said, lying back down.

"How about you scoot over," he said, "and Betsy and I will join you and Andy on the bed."

Both Andy and Betsy were thrilled with that solution. Debra didn't seem as enthusiastic, but she did as he asked. As soon as Betsy got close to Debra, she tried to get free of her father's hold so she could touch Debra.

"It's as if she knows you're sick," John said, watching Betsy.

"I'm not sick, at least not much. I'm sure it's just a touch of the flu. I felt it earlier this morning."

John glared at her. "And you didn't say anything? What's wrong with you, woman? You think you can just keep going?"

"That's what I've done in the past," she said, not looking at him.

"Didn't you have sick leave?"

"In a diner? I don't think so. If I can't be there, they'll hire someone who can."

Damn. The more he heard about Debra's previous life, the more he realized how tough she'd had to be. And he'd been so hard on her when she'd first come, not because of who she was, but because of who he was.

Gruffly, he said, "We don't operate that way here, honey. If you're sick, you just say you can't do your job and we'll take care of it until you can."

Debra looked at him, but she said nothing to him. Instead, she talked to the children. Andy played peekaboo with Betsy as Debra had taught him to. Betsy, now sitting in the circle of her daddy's arms next to Debra, leaned against John and gave a big belly laugh at Andy's antics.

Then she raised her hands to cover her eyes, just as Andy was doing.

"I've never seen her do that, Andy," Debra said. "Have you?"

"No, Mommy," Andy said between chuckles. Betsy

couldn't say peekaboo, but she could say boo. That had Andy in hysterics.

John couldn't help laughing, himself. He looked at Debra, smiling at the kids. "This is all because of you, Debra. I'm not sure my little girl would've learned to laugh if you hadn't come into her—our—lives."

Debra looked away from John. "Then I'm glad I'm here. Betsy should always be able to laugh."

"And me?" he asked quietly.

"I think everyone should be able to laugh."

"Good. I'm glad to hear it."

There was something between them, and John, for the life of him, could not figure out what it was. She wouldn't even make an effort to become friends. Of course, he wanted more than that, but it was a starting place.

He debated whether to let the doctor make his determination without any inside information, or to meet him at the door and let him know what was going on.

"What is it?" Debra asked, grabbing his attention. "You looked like you were making a big decision. If it affects me, I want to know. If Andy and I aren't wanted here, then we'll pack and be on our way!" she said, her voice angry.

Andy looked at his mother. "But, Mommy, you said we would live here for a long time. Has it been a long time, yet?" The little boy looked upset and John reached over to pat his shoulder.

"No, it definitely hasn't been a long time, Andy. You

and I have a date to ride out and see the baby calves real soon. I think I can talk your mommy into it."

"You do?" Andy asked in excitement.

"Yeah, I do. I know your mommy wants you to be happy. Right, Debra?"

She turned away, until they all heard the sound of the back door opening.

"We're back here, Tom," John called, and remained there with Debra and the kids.

Tom appeared in the doorway. "What are you doing? Working on the family plan?"

CHAPTER TWELVE

JOHN stood up and shook the doctor's hand. "Thanks for coming out, Tom."

"Good timing. It was before I started the clinic hours. Now, what's the problem?"

"My wife passed out this morning during breakfast."

Tom turned to stare at Debra. "You look pale. How are you feeling?"

Debra tried to sit up. With a look of confusion on her face she fell back on the pillow. "A—a little dizzy."

Tom looked at his friend. "John, why don't you take the kids into the living room while I give Debra an exam."

"I think—" John began, but both the doctor and Debra seemed opposed to whatever he thought. "Okay," he finally agreed, and picked up Betsy. "Come on, Andy, let's go play."

The little boy scooted off the bed and took John's hand, but his gaze was on his mother.

"It's all right, Andy. The doctor is going to fix me up. Then I'll be fine."

"Okay, Mommy."

Once the door was closed, Tom sat down on the bed.

"First question. Could you be pregnant?"

"No." Her cheeks were red and she didn't meet his gaze.

"How do you know?"

Debra glared at the doctor. "Because our marriage is one of convenience and we don't share a bedroom."

Tom's eyebrows rose, but he didn't pursue the topic. "Let me listen to your heart."

She tried to sit up, but the room spun around. She flopped back down on the pillow in frustration. "Why am I so light-headed?"

"Just lie still and let me listen to your heart." Tom placed his stethoscope on her chest. Then he looked at her eyes and sat up. "Okay, answer these questions. How many hours did you sleep last night?"

"Four. I usually get more, but lately, I've been trying to finish a quilt and—and I stayed up too late."

"What did you have for breakfast this morning?"

"I don't think I got around to breakfast. I was feeding Betsy and—"

"How about dinner last night?"

"I, uh, I was—"

"Debra, when was the last time you had a solid meal?"

She remained silent.

"Have you been losing weight?"

"A—a few pounds."

"Looks to me like more than a few. What I want to know is why. Is John driving you too hard? Do you need to have some time for yourself?"

"No! I can do my job."

"Not if you don't eat. You're a smart woman, Debra. If you skip meals and don't sleep enough, you get weak, light-headed. You should know that."

"I didn't realize— I was trying to finish the quilts."

"What's so important about these quilts?"

"I need to sell them at the fair."

"Did John ask you to do that?"

Her face turned bright red again. "No, it has nothing to do with John."

Tom nodded. She had the feeling he wasn't satisfied, but at least he stopped probing. "Well, you stay in bed. I'm going to have John bring you some breakfast. You are to eat every bit of it and stay in bed until after lunch, when you will again eat what he brings you. If you're feeling all right after a nap, then you can get up for dinner." He eyed her sharply. "Do you understand? If you don't follow my directions, you may become seriously ill and then you'll be of no use to anyone, least of all yourself."

John shook Tom's hand. "Thanks, Tom. I didn't think she'd believe me if I told her the same thing."

"You knew what was going on?"

"I'd noticed the weight loss, the paleness."

"Why didn't you do something?"

"We don't have that kind of relationship. Besides, she's a little hardheaded."

"She told me she'd been working so much to sell quilts. Excuse me, John, but I have to ask. Are you broke?"

"No. It's been tight, but since I sold the Escalade, I have enough money to make it until I sell the calf crop in the fall. I know about the quilts, but I don't know why. Did she tell you anything?"

"No. But I think you'd better find out and take care of whatever it is before she really hurts herself."

"Yeah, I will. Thanks again, Tom."

After Tom left, John settled the kids and went to the kitchen to put together a breakfast tray for Debra. He scrambled eggs and heated up leftover sausage, made some toast and poured a glass of milk.

Then he carried it to his bedroom. Debra opened her eyes as he came in. He set the tray down and picked up the extra pillows to prop her up.

"Thank you, John. I can feed myself."

"No, you can't. Until you get some food in you and some sleep, you can't do anything. I'm going to feed you, and we're going to talk seriously about what has been going on."

She looked away from him, as if afraid she might reveal a secret if he looked into her eyes.

"Here, take a bite. Now you can critique my cooking," he teased.

Gradually she relaxed as she ate her breakfast. John insisted she drink the entire glass of milk, as well as eat everything on the tray except the dishes. He threatened to call Tom back out if she didn't.

Though he'd hoped to talk to her, he recognized the sleepiness in her eyes as she finished the big meal. Without saying anything, he stood and took the extra pillows away. Then he kissed her cheek and told her to rest. She was asleep before he got to the door.

"Is Mommy okay?" Andy asked, a worried look on his face.

"She's fine, Andy. She ate a good breakfast and then fell asleep. She's been staying awake too late working on a quilt."

"I know," Andy said.

"Do you know why?" John asked. Then he chided himself. How desperate could he be, giving a three-year-old the third degree? "Never mind, Andy. We'll get things figured out. But today, you and Betsy are stuck with me."

"I'll help you, John. I can make Betsy laugh."

"I know, pal. You're the best at that. I'm going to finish cleaning up the kitchen. Then you can help me give Betsy her bath."

"Okay."

They spent the entire day together, John and the two children. They visited Debra at lunchtime and made sure she ate. Then Andy and Betsy joined her on the bed for their naps. Betsy slept between the other two, so she couldn't fall off the bed. John figured out dinner, using some shortcuts, like canned biscuits. The men might complain, but he would let them know they'd better be glad they didn't have to make dinner themselves.

He still hadn't had a heart-to-heart with Debra. He was eager to do so, but he wanted her to feel good before he pressed her for the truth. Otherwise, he'd feel like a brute, battering his wife.

When the men came in for dinner, no one complained at all. Afterward, John asked the men to clean the kitchen while Bill got the two children to bed.

John took Debra's dinner tray to his bedroom. She'd eaten well and slept most of the day. John figured another good meal should fix her up.

When he entered the room, she sat up.

"The room's not spinning? You must be feeling better."

"Yes, I am. I'm also feeling a little silly for letting things get in such bad shape."

"No need. We all make mistakes. Now, I prepared dinner, so I don't want to hear any complaints. Our normal great cook had to take a sick day, so I did my best."

"I'm sure it will be very good. I could've come to the table and saved you the trouble of bringing it to me."

"No. I want you to stay in bed all day today. Besides,

this will give us some time to talk. Something's wrong, and I want to know what it is."

"No, everything's fine." But she didn't sound convincing.

"Listen, Debra, I know I was rough on you when you first arrived. I didn't believe any woman could be selfless, a hard worker and really be sweet, too. But you're all of those things."

"No, I'm not."

"I believe you are." He took her spare hand in his. "Can't we start over?"

"Are you still planning on hiring a housekeeper in the fall?"

"Yeah, I should be able to do that."

She pulled her hand away and looked down. "Then we have nothing to talk about."

John tried to think through what they'd just said. Something didn't make sense. "My hiring a housekeeper is the sticking point? If I let you continue to do all the work and wear yourself out, you're happy?"

"If I don't work here, I'll just have to work somewhere else." She kept her head down, not giving him a chance to see her eyes.

"Wait! You're talking about an either/or situation? You think if the housekeeper comes, you'll be leaving? By my choice?"

She gave him a quick look, then ducked her head again.

"Are you crazy?" he demanded.

* * *

Debra thought she might be—crazy, that is. What he was saying wasn't computing in her head. She'd been working as hard as she could and everything had fallen apart today. Now, he wanted to talk about hiring a housekeeper.

"Debra, hiring a housekeeper doesn't mean I want you to go. I want you to stay, no matter what happens. We got married. I didn't hire you for the calving season. You're my wife."

"No, I'm not. We're not— We don't— I mean—"

He bent over and kissed her, and God help her, she let him.

He removed the tray and sat beside her. "You didn't pull away when I kissed you."

She shook her head, not looking at him.

He lifted her chin. "I hated the thought of marrying you because I thought you'd be like my first wife, even though Bill told me you'd be different. But it didn't take long to know that you weren't like Elizabeth. That first night at dinner, I couldn't believe all you'd managed to accomplish. But I didn't want to admit I was wrong. I apologize for that."

"It's all right."

"No, it's not, but it's in the past. I can't change my behavior then. But I want our marriage to work. I want it to be real. I want...I want you to love me like I love you. But I'm willing to give you time. And I was planning on hiring a housekeeper to make your life easier. Not to get rid of you."

"Oh," was Debra's only remark.

"So, will you stay?"

"I want to stay," she whispered, "but I don't know if— We're a package deal, me and Andy."

"Honey, Andy's not a problem. He's a great boy. He was the only positive thing I saw in our marriage because I didn't think I'd ever have a son of my own."

But she still felt wary. "What happens to Andy if you—we have a son?"

"Andy would have a little brother. If you're not going anywhere, he's not, either. He'll be my son as long as I live. Do you think he would like that?"

"Yes. He's never had a daddy. His father died before he was born, and my father died early, too."

"Then if he'll have me, I'll be his daddy. And if we have any other boys, they'll have a big brother to help them."

She nodded, still a solemn look on her face.

"What else?" he asked.

"You haven't questioned me about Betsy," she said.

He bent closer to give her another kiss, this one clinging a little longer. "Honey, I don't have to ask you about Betsy. You already treat her as if she were your own baby. She calls you Mama. You're the only mother she's ever known, except for those first two months of her life and it's a wonder she even survived. The best thing I ever did for my little girl was marry you."

"I love her so much. I'm glad you're not worried."

"Scoot over," he ordered. She scooted over as he aligned himself next to her and put his arm around her.

"How many kids do you think we should have?" he asked as he settled her body against his.

"I—I don't know."

"I think maybe four more. That would be six. I think we could handle six, don't you?"

Debra sat up and turned to look at him. "Six? You think that would be easy? We'll definitely need a housekeeper."

"That's my girl!" he said with a laugh. "I knew you had a fighting spirit. Meekness doesn't suit you!" He kissed her again.

She could get used to his kisses. A deep hunger grew in her and she slid her arms around his neck. As if he'd been waiting for that sign, he deepened the kiss. When they parted a couple of minutes later, they were both breathing heavily.

"Oh, Lordy, Debra Richey. I'm glad you're already my wife."

"Me, too," she said with a shy smile.

"Now we only have one other thing I can think of to discuss," he said. "What was the fascination with the quilts?"

"Oh."

"Come on, Deb, come clean."

"You said you were hiring a housekeeper in the fall.

I figured I needed to find a way to make money for me and Andy when we left. I was hoping to make four quilts before the fair."

"Lord have mercy, all the time you were killing yourself doing all the work I'd put on you and you still thought I'd turn you out without a penny? You must've thought me a monster!"

"No, John, I didn't, but I knew you were an angry man. And I understood why."

"I was. I won't deny that. But I'm not scum, honey. I owed you big-time. If things hadn't worked out, I'd have given you money, if nothing else."

"I didn't want your money," she whispered.

"Tell me what you wanted."

"You. That's all. You and Betsy."

"I already know Betsy's answer, and you have me, completely. Not only do I appreciate you, but I also love you. I love your unselfish spirit, your work ethic, your skills in the kitchen, your beautiful smile and, most of all, your warm heart. You took Betsy in right away. I'm glad I get to join her."

"Oh, you do. I want to make up to you for your past and build a future together."

He kissed her again, his hands wandering her body. When he finally pulled back, he rolled off the bed and stood.

"What are you doing?" she asked, startled.

"I'm heading out to one of the sofas in the living room."

"But this is your bed. I can go upstairs and—"

"No! I don't want you that far away. I'll stay out on the sofa as long as you want me to, but this is where I want you from now on."

"But, I—"

"Debra, I love you. But until you're ready, I'm going to wait. I owe you more than that. But I want you to be sure of what you want. So take some time. And let me know when you want me back in here." He turned to leave.

She only said one word, but it stopped him in his tracks. "Now."

He spun around, almost losing his balance. "What did you say?"

"I want you now, John. I don't want to be without you."

He stared at her. "You're sure?"

"Oh, yes. You won my heart when I realized how much you loved Betsy."

"I never knew fatherhood could lead to such happiness," he said with a grin as he returned to the bed.

EPILOGUE

THE church music swelled and the wedding march began. Debra, dressed in a beautiful white suit, walked slowly down the aisle with a big bouquet of flowers. She couldn't believe John had talked her into this display for their neighbors.

When she joined her husband at the altar, she expected Reverend Jackson to lead them through the wedding vows. Instead, John first kissed her. Then he turned to their audience.

"Ladies and gentlemen, we asked you here today to celebrate our nuptials. We were married last March, but it was at best a bare-bones ceremony. In truth, I married this woman in anger. I wasn't very nice to her. I had already been in one marriage that had been a colossal failure, partly due to me, though I was too angry to realize it at the time."

He squeezed Debra's hand. "God gave me an angel, and I scorned her. Today, I want you to know I'm remarrying this woman in love, not anger. I didn't want our children to remember that other wedding."

Then he turned to look at Andy and Betsy. "We've been blessed by two wonderful children who are a part of our union. Andy, can you and Betsy come up here, too?"

Having been coached by his new daddy, keeping a secret from his mom, Andy slipped off the church pew and took Betsy's hand. He and the toddler walked to his mom and dad. John handed Betsy to Debra and lifted Andy in his own strong arms. "We want you to join us in our happy union, and to announce the future arrival of a brother for Andy and Betsy."

Debra blushed. She'd told him that to marry again when she was obviously pregnant with their first child wasn't proper. He'd assured her it was the perfect thing to do.

Everyone clapped, showing they agreed with John.

Then he and Debra turned around and went through their vows again. And this time, John kissed his bride.

Afterward, they all adjourned to the café where a wedding cake and a lot of other food awaited their friends and neighbors.

Lucy put her arm around Debra. "I'm so happy for you two."

"Thank you, Lucy. And I can't tell you how happy I am that you're our housekeeper now. I was afraid John would find some stranger."

"Honeychild, all you had to do was ask. Baldy and

Aggie kept mc on because they were worried about me, but I landed in a bed of roses working for you and John."

Debra laughed. "Some bed of roses, with all the work you do! But we'll try not to let you get beaten down."

They were joined by John. "Hey, are you two plotting against me?"

"Never," Debra said with a smile that John felt all the way to his toes.

"How are you feeling, honey? Do you need to sit down?"

"No, I'm fine. Lucy and I were just talking about how happy we are."

"Did that have anything to do with your uncle Bill?" John asked, an innocent expression on his face that didn't fool either lady.

Lucy turned a bright red.

Debra chided her husband. "Behave, John. You shouldn't tease Lucy."

"No, of course not," he said with a chuckle. "But I'll admit I'm enjoying watching Bill go through the throes of love."

"You're not helping the situation," Debra protested.

"Okay, I'll change the subject." He raised his champagne glass and tapped it against her juice cup. "Let's talk about how much I love you." Then he showed her how much with a kiss.

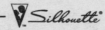

SPECIAL EDITION™

**Experience the "magic" of
falling in love at Halloween with
a new *Holiday Hearts* story!**

UNDER HIS SPELL

by KRISTIN HARDY

October 2006

Bad-boy ski racer J. J. Cooper can get any
woman he wants—except Lainie Trask.
Lainie's grown up with him and vows that
nothing he says or does will change her mind.
But J.J.'s got his eye on Lainie, and when
he moves into her neighborhood and into her
life, she finds herself falling under his spell....

THE PART-TIME WIFE

by *USA TODAY* bestselling author

Maureen Child

Abby Talbot was the belle of Eastwick society;
the perfect hostess and wife. If only her
husband were more attentiive. But when
she sets out to teach him a lesson and files
for divorce, Abby quickly learns her husband's
true identity...and exposes them to scandals
and drama galore!

On sale October 2006 from Silhouette Desire!

*Available wherever books are sold,
including most bookstores, supermarkets,
discount stores and drug stores.*

Those sexy Irishmen are back!

Bestselling author

Kate Hoffmann

is joining the Harlequin Blaze line—and she's
brought her bestselling Temptation miniseries,
THE MIGHTY QUINNS, with her.
Because these guys are definitely Blaze-worthy....

All Quinn males, past and present, know the legend
of the first Mighty Quinn. And they've all been
warned about the family curse—that the only thing
capable of bringing down a Quinn is a woman.
Still, the last three Quinn brothers never guess
that lying low could be so sensually satisfying....

The Mighty Quinns: Marcus, on sale October 2006
The Mighty Quinns: Ian, on sale November 2006
The Mighty Quinns: Declan, on sale December 2006

Don't miss it!

Available wherever Harlequin books are sold.

If you enjoyed what you just read,
then we've got an offer you can't resist!

Take 2 bestselling love stories FREE!

Plus get a FREE surprise gift!

Clip this page and mail it to Silhouette Reader Service™

IN U.S.A.	IN CANADA
3010 Walden Ave.	P.O. Box 609
P.O. Box 1867	Fort Erie, Ontario
Buffalo, N.Y. 14240-1867	L2A 5X3

YES! Please send me 2 free Silhouette Romance® novels and my free surprise gift. After receiving them, if I don't wish to receive anymore, I can return the shipping statement marked cancel. If I don't cancel, I will receive 4 brand-new novels every month, before they're available in stores! In the U.S.A., bill me at the bargain price of $3.57 plus 25¢ shipping and handling per book and applicable sales tax, if any*. In Canada, bill me at the bargain price of $4.05 plus 25¢ shipping and handling per book and applicable taxes**. That's the complete price and a savings of at least 10% off the cover prices—what a great deal! I understand that accepting the 2 free books and gift places me under no obligation ever to buy any books. I can always return a shipment and cancel at any time. Even if I never buy another book from Silhouette, the 2 free books and gift are mine to keep forever.

210 SDN DZ7L
310 SDN DZ7M

Name	(PLEASE PRINT)	
Address	Apt.#	
City	State/Prov.	Zip/Postal Code

Not valid to current Silhouette Romance® subscribers.

Want to try two free books from another series?
Call 1-800-873-8635 or visit www.morefreebooks.com.

* Terms and prices subject to change without notice. Sales tax applicable in N.Y.
** Canadian residents will be charged applicable provincial taxes and GST.
   All orders subject to approval. Offer limited to one per household.
   ® are registered trademarks owned and used by the trademark owner or its licensee.

SROM04R   ©2004 Harlequin Enterprises Limited

SILHOUETTE *Romance*®

COMING NEXT MONTH

#1834 RESCUED BY MR. RIGHT—Shirley Jump
Victoria Blackstone is ready to change her life and for once put herself first. But she isn't sure she has the courage to do it alone. Noah McCarty has hit the road to escape his damaged past. When he becomes stranded, Victoria comes to his rescue, and he is bowled over by her innocence and charm.

#1835 HER MILLIONAIRE BOSS—Jennie Adams
Chrissy Gable is determined not to be charmed by her handsome new boss, but soon she finds herself tempted to stay after hours with Nate Barrett. Nate is struggling to understand his attraction to his quirky PA, but knows he must keep his distance; Chrissy, with her warm heart, deserves *real* love—the type that lasts.

#1836 FOUND: HIS FAMILY—Nicola Marsh
A successful businesswoman and single mom, Aimee has everything in life she wants—especially her little boy, Toby. But Toby is sick, and Aimee now needs the person she thought she would never see again, his father, Jed. When Jed left five years ago he hadn't known Aimee was pregnant. Now Jed is determined to make up for lost time.

#1837 O'REILLY'S BRIDE—Trish Wylie
Sean O'Reilly has become so close to his colleague Maggie Sullivan that he's beginning to imagine their friendship can lead to more. Only now—bizarrely—she's backed off. And, even more strangely, she's started looking for love on the Internet! Well, if Sean can't beat them, he'll have to join them....